WHERE'S THE VACATION?

Also by Dawn Chalker

BEAR ME IN MIND

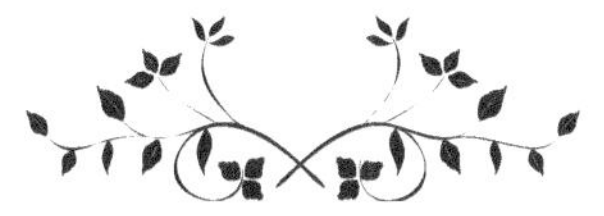

Where's the Vacation?

Short Stories

Dawn Chalker

Hepatica Books

Cover design by Dawn Chalker and Peter Solenberger
Author photo by Briana Chalker

Library of Congress Control Number: 2023908115

ISBN 979-8-218-20183-8

Hepatica Books
Traverse City, Michigan
hepaticabooks.com

To all of my family members with whom
I have enjoyed family vacations.

CONTENTS

Black Cat Ghost — 1

Let's go Sea-Kayaking — 24

Mystery at the French Cathedral — 39

Atelihai (Hello or Welcome) — 60

Family Vacation Deluxe — 73

The Great Dragon Woods — 90

Up in a Balloon — 122

1920s Petoskey — 133

Aloha — 154

A Superior Vacation — 175

Virtual Vacation — 194

The Best Summer Vacation Ever — 212

Black Cat Ghost

Paige looked at the bridge that spanned a wide river flowing toward the ocean. If you crossed the bridge, where could you go?

Her grandpa parked the car on the street. "Well, here we are." He opened the car door and got out.

"Is there a beach here?" Paige stepped out of the car and looked around. This was Florida, after all.

"Just follow the river. This is the Apalachicola River. Goes right down to the Gulf of Mexico." Grandpa gestured to the wide river that winked in the sunlight through the trees. He opened the trunk and grasped a large black suitcase and a plastic bag full of fishing rods. He set them beside the car and pulled out two more suitcases. "I can feel that big fish pulling on my line now." He grinned.

Paige wrinkled her nose. The river did smell like fish.

"There are many beautiful beaches nearby, I think." Grandma tugged out a large tote bag with yarn spilling over the top. "Before we leave to go home, we will be sure to spend a day or two at one of them."

'Great." Paige turned and looked up at the Thompson Inn. A round cupola perched on top of a blue, three-story house. White wooden rocking chairs lined the veranda. In one chair sat a sleek black cat, who gazed at her through slitted eyes.

"They have a black cat. Do you think that's unlucky?"

"What's that?" Grandma picked up her suitcase.

"The black cat. Do you think it's unlucky?"

"No, of course not. Cats are not unlucky."

Paige picked up her suitcase and tote bag. When she looked back at the porch, the cat was gone.

Her grandparents carried their luggage into the Inn. Behind them, Paige climbed the steps, opened the double glass doors, and crossed the dark plank floor to the polished wooden counter. A large ceramic lamp with a fringed pink lampshade sat next to a vase of yellow tulips. An old-fashioned brass mailbox on a pedestal stood at one end. A large man dressed in khakis and a long-sleeved polo leaned on the counter.

The young woman behind the counter pointed to a map. "The best fishing is across the bridge and down about there. If you walk along the river, you can find places to hire a boat or take a charter boat.

The man nodded, took a pen out of his shirt pocket, and drew a circle on the map. He put X's on the map where the woman pointed.

A yellow tabby cat snoozed beside the lamp with one large paw draped lazily over the counter. Paige gently stroked its thick, warm fur.

"He likes to be rubbed behind the ears."

She turned and looked into the brown eyes of a tall, slim boy. About her own age, maybe. "What's his name?"

"Mr. C."

"What's the C for?"

"Cuddles. My sister named him when he was a kitten, but after he grew up, he wanted a cooler image. So now I call him Mr. C."

"Hi there, Mr. C." Paige rubbed his head. "What's the other cat's name?"

"Other cat?" The boy squinted his eyes and looked at her.

"The black cat that was sleeping on the porch."

He paused for a long moment.

"Well, does it have a name?"

The boy shrugged and turned away. "Must have been a stray."

"Hello, young lady. We have a reservation." Grandpa smiled at the clerk.

She smiled back, looked up the reservation name, and handed him two keys. "Your room is up the stairs and to the right. My brother Dylan will help you carry these bags up to room number 4." The young woman at the counter pointed to two bags sitting beside the counter and gestured to the boy who had been talking to Paige.

Dylan looked at Paige and rolled his eyes. He picked up the bags and climbed the stairs two at a time. Upstairs, Dylan led them down the hall to a corner room and set down the bags. "This is number 4. Enjoy your stay." He looked at Paige and gave her a shy smile. "You should visit the Chocolate Shoppe. Best chocolate-covered strawberries you'll ever eat."

"Thanks for the suggestion." Paige smiled.

"Thanks, young man." Grandpa put a dollar into Dylan's hand. Dylan nodded his thanks and went back down the stairs.

Grandpa turned the key and opened the door. They entered a room wallpapered in marine blue with tiny white flowers. Three tall, double hung windows lined one wall, with a view of the bridge that spanned the river across the street. In one corner a door led out to a small closed-in porch.

"You can have the porch room all to yourself." Grandma pointed toward the open door.

Paige took her suitcase and tote bag onto the porch. She set her things onto a day bed made up with a colorful quilt on top. There was a small rocking chair in the corner and a small dresser next to it. Windows along two sides provided a view of the river.

"Look at that view. The sun is still high in the sky. Can't wait to catch some of those fish." Grandpa fingered his fishing pole.

"You go on, then." Grandma patted his arm. "Paige and I will entertain ourselves."

Grandpa changed into his fishing clothes, grabbed his gear, and walked down the street.

"Let's check out the stores and see what this town looks like." Grandma picked up her purse and Paige followed her out of their room.

Outside, Paige admired the palm trees that lined the street. Just a block from the Thompson Inn, they discovered the town. People sauntered down the street, entered the stores, or sat on the benches around a grassy square licking ice cream cones. The square was bordered by bushes of colorful flowers.

"Hibiscus and bougainvillea," Grandma said. "That market area seems to have a lot of different stores. Oh, look, there's a fiber store."

While her grandmother looked at all the yarn available in the fiber store, Paige went inside a store that sold sea sponges. On one wall was a poster that described how Apalachicola was once a sponge capital. Colorful pictures showed some of the different sponges that people could find. She didn't know there were so many different sponges. In a clothing store, she found a tee shirt with the word Apalachicola embroidered on the front of it.

"Are you visiting here?" The young woman who rang up her purchase smiled at her.

"For a week. My grandpa likes to fish."

"The fishing is very good around here. He will enjoy that."

Paige nodded

"Enjoy your stay."

Paige turned and smiled. "Thanks."

Back at the inn, Grandma went upstairs to take a nap. Paige sat in a rocking chair on the veranda. She sketched a picture of the bridge across the street, and read a few pages of a book she was supposed to finish before the end of spring break. She texted her two best friends, who she was sure were having more fun than she was, and watched a YouTube video about a cat that could open doors. She drank a glass of lemonade and ate two cookies that the young woman from the counter brought out and sat on a nearby table.

When her grandpa returned, Paige was glad to see he hadn't caught any fish. What would he do with them? He couldn't just set a pail of them in their room.

"Great fishing. Just getting started today. Checking the lay of the water. Tomorrow I'm going out on one of those charter boats. Plan to catch a big one. Lots of ones to fish for: speckled trout, flounder, red snapper. Can't wait."

Paige wrinkled her nose.

"Don't worry. I'm not planning to bring the fish back here. The boat crew takes care of cleaning and wrapping the fish. We'll pick them up before we leave."

"Did you two have a good time, a chance to relax?" Grandpa patted Paige's shoulder.

Paige shrugged. "I guess."

"Well, I'm starving. How about you, Paige? Let's check out the dining room and see what's good to eat. I'll just run upstairs and change my clothes and meet you there."

Paige and her grandmother went inside and into the dining room, which was next to the reception area.

"Sit anywhere." The woman who had been at the front desk handed them menus as they entered the dining room. They sat at a table by a window that looked out on the back vegetable garden. At the empty table next to them, Dylan glanced at her as he stacked dirty dishes on a large tray.

It was all-you-can-eat fish night. Paige chose a salad and a veggie burger, and then decided to have dessert. "I'm going to sit outside on the porch." Paige forked the last bite of key lime pie and stood up.

"Don't leave the porch, though. We'll be out in a minute. Save us a seat." Grandma took a sip of her coffee.

Out on the porch, Paige breathed in the cool, salty ocean air. The sun spread fingers of light on the river as darkness crept in slowly. She heard laughter around the corner of the porch, but all the chairs on this side were empty.

In the dim light, Paige spotted the black cat sitting on the porch railing a few yards away, watching her, unblinking.

"Here, kitty, kitty." Paige walked a bit closer, knelt down, and stretched out her hand. The cat looked at her, jumped down, and trotted across the street. A car zipped around the corner, and Paige gasped as the cat appeared to leap right between the tires. She hurried across the street, hoping he was still alive. When she reached the other side, the cat turned and trotted off down the street. Paige followed him two blocks to the the bridge. She looked away and then back. No cat.

"What are you doing out here in the dark? Could be dangerous." Paige whirled around at the sound of a voice behind her.

"Sorry, didn't mean to scare you." Dylan grinned.

"I'm not scared. You just surprised me." Paige backed up a step.

"You look like you've seen a ghost."

"Just looking at the bridge. You shouldn't sneak up on people in the dark like that." Paige looked at Dylan. "Didn't you carry our bags upstairs?"

"Yeah. My mom owns the Inn."

"Is it fun?"

"What?"

"Working at the Inn?"

"Not really."

"Does your dad work here, too?"

"He's long gone."

"So, what does everyone do around here?"

"Not much."

"Doesn't it get pretty boring?"

"Probably. Some of the tourists are interesting, though. I'd better get back to the kitchen. It'll be time to clean up from dinner. Come on, I'll walk you back. This is a sleepy town, but you shouldn't wander around by yourself."

"I can take care of myself."

"Sure. We could go around the back way, and you could walk around the side of the veranda to meet your grandparents. In case they wondered where you were or something."

"Okay. I wouldn't want them to worry or anything."

In the morning, Paige stepped out onto the veranda. She breathed in the salty air and felt the warm sun on her shoulders. When she walked around the corner of the veranda, she found Dylan sitting on the back steps with baskets of plump, red strawberries stacked beside him. Dylan tossed a strawberry into a large, metal bowl. It made a pinging sound.

"I can't believe there are fresh strawberries in April!"

He looked up at her. "Don't they have strawberries where you're from?"

"In June. Michigan berries are the best."

"Try one of these."

Paige popped it into her mouth. "Yum. Want some help?"

"Sure, if you feel like it. Tourists are getting strawberry shortcake tonight."

Paige sat down on the step next to Dylan and hulled several berries, then turned to Dylan. "So, have you ever seen any ghosts here at the inn? It's so old and all, I mean."

Dylan laughed. "Tourists love a good ghost at an old inn like this. No, I've never seen a human ghost."

"Are there other kinds?"

"Do you think animals can have ghosts?"

"Sure. Maybe they died mysteriously or violently or something."

"Like cats, maybe?"

Paige's eyes widened. "Black cats, maybe?"

"Yeah." Dylan paused.

"You don't mean…"

"That black cat you saw. He's not a stray."

"Oh, come on. You're teasing me."

Dylan shook his head. "There was this old guy, Edward Nantucket. Well, maybe fifties anyway. He was a friend of my grandma. She called him Eddie. He had a houseboat on the river that he stayed in all the time. He used to buy and sell things up and down the river. Started telling some people, like my grandma, that he was going to get rich. Then one night a couple of years ago, his boat disappeared. Two days later, someone found it sunk along the shore of the river. Over by the park." Dylan pointed across the river on the other side of the bridge. "Never found his body."

"What does that have to do with a black cat?"

"He had a black cat named Artemis. Cat lived on the boat with him. Edward loved that cat. Took him everywhere, even to the bar."

"Did he drink?"

"Edward?"

"No, Artemis."

Dylan laughed. "Don't know about that. But the cat never showed up after the boat sunk, except last year on the anniversary of Edward's death."

"When did Edward die?"

"April 12." Dylan gave her a long look.

"Today is April 12."

"Yeah."

"And you saw him?"

"I did."

Paige was silent for a minute, thinking. "Do you think the cat wants something?"

"Probably."

"I saw him last night going across the bridge."

"Me, too." Dylan jumped up. A couple of strawberries rolled down the steps. Dylan picked them up. Hulled them, and put them in the bowl. "Maybe he wants us to follow him."

"You think so?" Paige looked up at him.

"Of course. He must want to show us something."

"Us?"

"Well, sure. You can't go alone."

"You really think we can follow a ghost cat?"

"Sure, why not? We've got to do it tonight, though. I only saw him once last year."

"Okay."

"What about your grandparents?"

"I can manage."

"I'll meet you in the lobby at 11:00 tonight."

Paige nodded. "I'll be there."

Paige kept her clothes on and went to bed early, before her grandparents came upstairs. She lay in the daybed with the sheet pulled up to her chin. When they both began snoring, she guessed they were asleep. She slid out of bed, still dressed in her clothes, and tiptoed to the door. Slowly, she turned the lock, edged open the door, and carefully stepped into the hallway.

Rose-colored lights along the walls cast dim shadows across the dark wooden floor. She glanced down the hall toward room 3 and across the hall to rooms 1 and 2. All was quiet. Paige stepped lightly down the staircase. When she put her foot on one of the steps, it gave a soft creak. She stepped over that one and set her foot carefully on the next one down.

Light from the streetlamps crept through the shuttered windows, casting stripes upon the floor of the empty lobby.

"Hey," a whispered voice said. Paige jumped. Dylan stood beside her in the dim light.

"Let's go out the back door. Step where I do so the floorboards don't creak. I know where all the creaky ones are."

Outside, at the back of the veranda, they looked up and down the street. A car door slammed, and a radio played softly, but the street appeared deserted.

Something soft brushed against Paige's legs, and she covered her mouth so as not to scream. She looked down at Mr. C. who rubbed in and out of her legs.

"Do you think Mr. C. can see the black cat?"

Dylan shrugged. "Cats can see things people can't."

They hurried down the steps, around the corner of the inn, and across the street. They glanced back at the darkened building. A cool spring breeze tickled Paige's hair, and waves slapped the pilings underneath a nearby dock.

"Do you see the black cat?" Dylan whispered.

"No." Paige peered across the bridge. She grabbed Dylan's arm. "There." She pointed to a dark shape that trotted down the street ahead of them. Running quietly, they followed the shadowy form.

Crossing the bridge, they came to the entrance of the park on the other side of the river. Hanging from a chain stretched across the arched entrance was a sign: "Park closed at 10:00 pm. NO ENTRANCE."

"Do you think he went in there?" Paige squinted into the dark.

"Maybe." Dylan held down the chain as they both stepped over it. He pulled a flashlight out of his backpack and shone it around the edges of the park. Leaves rustled, and two eyes glowed at them from the bushes. They followed the cat down the path along the river.

"There!" Dylan pointed to a rusted-out boat frame where the black cat sat, staring silently.

"Don't startle him." Paige edged closer to Dylan.

"One step at a time."

Paige nodded and stepped one foot closer. The cat re-mained where he was, as they moved closer to the boat. Then he jumped down and dashed toward an old dock. Paige and Dylan hurried after him.

"Yikes!" Paige gasped. Sitting on the dock was the shadowy figure of an old man. Looking down, he gently stroked the cat's head. His hand passed right through the cat.

"Is that him?" Paige shivered. Ghosts of cats were one thing, but people ghosts were scary!

Dylan nodded. "Maybe this isn't such a good idea after all." The ghost of Edward looked up and stared straight at them with hollow eyes. Slowly, the figure stood up and reached out a hand.

Paige grabbed Dylan's arm, and they raced back in the direction they had come from. Paige could feel a cold breeze behind her and ran faster. Suddenly, she stopped, and Dylan reached out his arms to avoid running into her. She turned to look behind them. No one there.

"We have to go back. Otherwise, we're letting the cat down." Paige touched Dylan's arm.

"Okay. If you're sure about this." He reached for her hand, and they crept back to the boat. Edward was still standing, watching. Paige shivered. Edward turned away, limped to the end of the dock, and ambled off towards a grove of trees. Artemis trotted after him. Without making a sound, Dylan and Paige followed them.

As they got closer to the trees, they saw a shovel propped against an old weeping willow with branches that gently brushed the river. Edward nodded as he disappeared into the trees. Artemis sat and watched them.

"Maybe we're supposed to dig for something," Dylan whispered.

Dylan walked closer and touched the shovel. "This is real anyway. You keep an eye out for Edward. If he comes back, I'm out of here."

Dylan pushed the shovel into the soft, moist dirt.

"How do we know where exactly to dig?"

"X marks the spot, I guess." Dylan pointed to two sticks that were crossed like an X. He plunged the shovel into the dirt and kept digging until he heard a light thud. "I think I've hit something."

He uncovered a metal box and knelt down to brush off the dirt. Paige knelt beside him and helped scrape off the dirt around it. Dylan looked at Paige and raised his eyebrows.

"Guess we might as well open it."

The box had an old-fashioned hook and eye closure. It was slightly rusted, but Dylan forced it open. Inside was a cloth sack tied with a piece of twine at the top.

"What do you think might be in there? Nothing gross, I hope."

Dylan shook his head as he untied the twine. The knot was old, and it took him a few minutes to get it loosened. He pulled open the bag, looked inside, and whistled softly. He handed the bag to Paige, and she looked in. The bag was filled with gold coins. On top of them was a locket. She reached in and pulled it out. She slid her thumbnail beneath the lid and opened it. Inside was a picture of a young woman. "She's very pretty." She handed it to Dylan.

"Wow! It looks like my grandma when she was young. I've seen pictures of her that look like that." He turned it over. "To Edward. Love, Annie. That's my grandma's name."

"Do you think he was in love with her?"

"She talked about him a lot."

"I wonder why they didn't get married, then."

"Maybe Edward wasn't really the marrying kind. Anyway, he died and that was that."

Paige had forgotten all about Edward and the black cat. She looked up. The cat was still watching. He blinked at her and then turned and disappeared.

"He's leaving."

Dylan looked at the empty spot where the cat had been. "I guess that's what he wanted us to do for him."

"Do you think we'll ever see him again?"

"I don't know much about ghost cats. But at least he got what he wanted."

Paige nodded. "I'm glad we helped him."

"Me, too." Dylan covered up the hole he had dug and set the shovel up against the tree. He carried the box as they walked quickly back to the park entrance and sat down on a bench to look at it again. Paige shook the coins into her lap, and they counted them.

"What should we do with the coins and the locket?" Paige looked at the box.

"Let's take it to my grandma. I'd like you to meet her. She isn't very well these days, but she'll be glad to meet you."

"I'd like to meet her. We'd better get back to the inn, though, before someone realizes we're gone."

"Are you going to tell your grandparents?"

"Maybe."

The half-moon glowed in a midnight blue sky as they walked back to the inn in silence. The river slapped gently against the pilings as they crossed the bridge. Paige expected to see the black cat waiting for them, but the rocking chairs on the veranda were empty. She slid quietly into her room and beneath the covers, listening to the rhythmic snoring of her grandparents.

Early the next morning, Paige got up, dressed, and hurried downstairs. At the bottom of the stairs, she noted that Dylan's sister was already standing at the counter, talking to an elderly couple.

"Have you seen Dylan?"

She looked at Paige, puzzled. "He's in the kitchen, I think."

Paige cracked open the kitchen door and waited for Dylan to turn around. He nodded and finished arranging strawberries on a fruit platter. He followed her out to the porch and picked up the box they had dug up.

"Let's go." They walked down a tree-lined street for several blocks and turned right. Dylan stopped in front of a two-story blue house with porches across both stories. Newly painted white railings lined the porches. The lower porch steps led to a front door with glass panels on either side.

"What am I going to say exactly? This will be kind of weird, don't you think?" Dylan frowned.

"Kind of. Let's just tell her the truth. She's your grandma. She'll understand."

"I guess. Let's go."

They walked up the steps. Dylan opened the door and called. "Grandma, you home?"

A small woman with chin-length gray hair came out, wiping her hands on a dish cloth.

"Hey, Dylan. Guess you must have smelled my chocolate chip cookies." She gave him a big hug. "And who's this?" She smiled at Paige.

"This is Paige. She's staying at the Inn. We have something to tell you."

"This sounds serious. Come tell me over warm cookies." She led them into the kitchen. They pulled out chairs and sat at the table. She placed a plate of cookies in front of them. "So, what's on your mind."

"Well, you remember Edward," Dylan began.

"Yes, of course. No one who knew Edward could ever forget him. Why?" Grandma's eyes teared up.

"I know this sounds strange, but we saw his cat."

"Artemis," she whispered. "What do you mean you saw his cat?"

"A ghost of his cat. Anyway, the cat seemed to want us to follow him, so we did, and he led us to the ghost of Edward." Dylan continued, hoping to get the story out all at once. "Edward sort of showed us where to dig, and we found this." He held out the box.

"I don't understand. I know people have talked about seeing Artemis and Edward, but those are just stories." His grandma looked at Dylan and then at Paige. "Aren't they?"

"Look in the box and see what you think."

She opened the box and gazed at the locket and the coins inside.

"I knew he didn't forget me," she said. "I don't really understand, but this means the world to me."

Later that morning, Dylan placed Paige's suitcase in the trunk of the car. "Well, send me a postcard from Michigan."

"I will." She looked up at Dylan. "And you can write and tell me all about the tourists at the inn."

"Sure. They're not always so interesting as this." He looked at her intently.

Paige smiled. "I'm sure the people who work here are always interesting."

"Maybe you'll be back by here sometime."

"I hope so. Or maybe you'll come visit Michigan to see what strawberries taste like in June."

"I might at that."

Paige got into the backseat of the car. She looked back at Dylan as the car pulled away from the curb. Watching him climb the steps up to the inn, she saw Mr. C. lying in one of the rockers.

"He's smiling," Paige thought. Maybe he had been seeing Artemis all along. Cats are like that sometimes.

FUN FACTS:

Are black cats unlucky?

Definitely not. In Japan, black fortune cats represent good luck. There are many kinds of black cats, some with short hair and some with long hair. The author of this story lived with a smart, affectionate, and playful black cat for 18 years.

What are sea sponges?

Sea sponges are one of the world's simplest multicellular living organisms. Even though they look like plants, they are animals. They grow, reproduce, and survive in ways similar to plants, without a central nervous system, digestive system or circulatory system.

Sponges come in many shapes and colors and range in size from 1 cm to 2 meters. Thousands of different species of sponges live in the world.

(Geokansas.ku.edu/sponges)

Let's go Sea-Kayaking

Justin and Blake sat on the porch playing games on their phones. Without putting down his phone, Blake said, "Dad's going to drop us off at the kayak place. He made arrangements for Pete to take us sea-kayaking this afternoon.

Justin looked at his cousin Blake, who was only a few months older but already an inch taller than Justin. "Sea-kayaking. In one of those boats where you sit on the floor and paddle. Right out on the ocean." Justin imagined waves ten feet high looming over his kayak.

"You don't sit on the floor exactly. There's a seat in it, and you work the rudder with your feet, to steer. We'll be on the ocean, but there are plenty of islands, so it's pretty protected." Blake grinned. "The waves don't get *really* big out there."

"No problem. Sounds pretty easy." Growing up in Nebraska, he hadn't spent much time on the ocean. But how hard could it be?

When Blake's dad dropped them off at the kayak rental, Justin and Blake climbed the steps and entered the office in a log cabin. While Blake walked up to the counter, Justin looked at a rack of brochures: kayaking on Maine rivers and the Atlantic Ocean, fishing trips, sunset sailing.

"My Dad reserved a couple of kayaks for my cousin and me." Blake told the woman at the counter.

She smiled. "Yeah, I know your dad. And you look like him."

Blake shrugged. He heard that a lot.

"Head on down to the dock. Pete will meet you there and get you set up."

Blake and Justin walked outside and down to the dock. Justin stared out at the big expanse of ocean. Sunlight winked off small waves in the distance.

Their guide, a wiry older man with curly hair and a goatee, shook hands with them. "All right, time to get you guys outfitted. The name's Pete and I'll be taking you out around the islands. I've taught middle school science to boys about your age."

"We're 14." Blake wanted to make it clear that they were no longer in middle school.

"You taught science, and now you're guiding kayaks?" Justin tried to picture his science teacher, Mrs. Rudd, in a kayak. He couldn't see it.

Pete laughed. "Been kayaking out here for years. Here's your skirts, boys." He laughed and handed them each a circular piece of vinyl that flared out at the bottom like a skirt. "Just kidding. Step into it like this, pull it up about chest high. Pull the strap snugly across."

Blake pulled up the one Pete handed to him and tightened the Velcro across his chest. Justin stepped into one and pulled it up. It felt awkward.

"Like this." Pete reached over and helped him adjust it. He handed them each a life vest. "You boys vacationing here in Maine?"

"Kind of," said Justin.

"I live near here," said Blake. "I go to school in Blue Hill

"So, this kayaking stuff is old hat to you."

"Been kayaking with my parents and little sister a few times."

"How about you, Justin?"

"Justin and me are cousins. He's visiting for a week from Nebraska. I'm showing him a Maine vacay." He grinned.

"I have been out fishing a few times with my grandpa. He took me kayaking on the river. My mom was on the swim team, so I took swimming lessons at the Y." It wasn't like he'd never been around the water, Justin thought. It's just that the ocean was different. Currents and tides and sharks and stuff.

Pete led them down to the kayaks stacked along the water. Justin tried not to waddle like a penguin, all bulky with that skirt thing and a life vest.

"This should be about right. Hold your arm up over your head." Pete stood a paddle up that just reached the tip of Justin's fingers. "That looks about the right length." He handed the paddle to Justin. Then he did the same for Blake.

"Now, some safety info. Stick together, but not too close. Stay clear of speedboats, though they really should stay clear of you. And if you should flip all the way over, so your head is underwater, beat on the bottom of your kayak to alert your companions. No one will hear you if you yell. Pull the tip of your skirting off the hook and slip out."

Flip over? Justin didn't see how he could possibly unhook this skirt thing from the kayak in order to slide out before he drowned. Would he remember to beat on the bottom of the boat if his head was underwater? Maybe Pete was just trying to scare them. It couldn't happen very often, right?

Pete held the kayak as Justin stepped into it. "Rock gently back and forth from your hips, and you won't tip over." Pete swayed back and forth to demonstrate. Then he pushed the kayak away from the shore. "Just practice paddling around this little bay. Once we all get in, we'll head out over there." Pete pointed across the bay.

Justin stared "over there." It looked far away and over open water. Power boats whizzed through there pretty fast. Justin tried not to think how fast he'd have to paddle if he was in the path of one. He had a few minutes to practice while he waited for Blake and Pete. But he didn't want to get too far away from shore.

Justin balanced the paddle with his hands near the center, the way Pete had shown him. Paddling straight on wasn't too hard, but the rudder was a little tricky. If he pushed with the wrong foot, he turned in the direction he didn't want to go. He looked up and saw a boat moored ahead of him, not too far away. "Whoa!" Justin muttered as the kayak spun too far to the right. He pushed more gently on the rudder and the kayak straightened its course. By the time Pete and Blake paddled out to him, he was starting to relax a little.

"We're going to head straight out. I'll be watching out for power boats, so we can stay out of their way. Just stick close to me until you get the hang of it." Pete pointed and paddled off easily.

Blake padded with a strong stroke, almost passing Pete. As Justin got into a comfortable rhythm, he looked around. The early morning sun washed the houses and buildings clustered around the bay in pale gold, but it hadn't yet warmed the cool air. Paddling was beginning to warm him up, though.

Pete paddled across the channel, skillfully timing their interactions to miss the power boats passing through. Over there turned out to be an island. They paddled along the shoreline to the other side of the island, where there was another wide channel to cross.

Justin shrugged his shoulders to get out the stiffness. A monstrous power boat roared past them. Justin rolled from the hips so as not to overturn his kayak as it rocked back and forth in the wake of the boat.

"Hey, Tim! Slow down!" Pete shouted at the speedboat. Pete waited until Blake and Justin were next to him. "That dumb kid is going to run into someone someday. I don't know why his parents let him out alone." Pete shook his head. "Come on, stick close. Most of the power boats are good about giving us the right of way."

After crossing the wide channel, they entered a narrow slice of water between two islands. Justin breathed in the salty, fresh air. He felt much more relaxed, not having to watch for speedboats. Their paddles dipped silently in and out of the water. A bald eagle soared overhead and landed in a large nest on top of a pine tree.

"Look." Blake pointed to a spot on the left side of Justin's kayak. Justin squinted in the sun and saw two brown balls bobbing along the surface.

"Seals," Blake said.

Justin paddled closer. As he neared them, he glimpsed big black eyes and whiskers just before they slid below the surface of the water. "Way cool," said Justin and grinned.

"We'll stop here for lunch." Pete paddled his kayak to a patch of sand on another island. Blake and Justin let their kayaks drift in. They lifted their day packs out of the hatches of their kayaks and followed Pete. Tall grass that they could barely see over crowded the narrow path. They climbed over several boulders and stood on a stone ledge. Looking over the edge, they gazed down at a smooth pond several feet below them.

"Abandoned quarry. Let's have a swim before we eat." Pete pulled off his T-shirt and dove into the water, barely making a splash. "Come on in," Pete called as he swam off across the pond.

Blake tossed his tee shirt onto the rocks and dove in. Not as graceful as Pete, but decent, Justin thought. Justin watched Pete and Blake swim strongly toward the other side.

Blake waved. "Hey, come on in. The water's great. You won't get cold."

Justin breathed in, out. His diving had not been too successful at the Y. He held his breath and jumped off, feet first. When he hit the water with a big splash, he went all the way under. He surfaced and did a crawl stroke across the pond to the ledge on the other side.

"Looks like you can swim anyway," Pete said.

"Not too good at diving, though."

Pete shrugged. "Just need some practice, that's all."

"Yeah, maybe."

They sat silently for several minutes and watched a pair of loons glide across the pond. Pete stood up. "I'm hungry. Let's eat." He dove in and swam back to the other side. Justin almost kept up with Blake, as they followed Pete

On the other side, they all climbed out onto the rocks and dried off. Two ham sandwiches and several chocolate chip cookies later, Justin stretched out on the rocky ledge. Heat from the sun-warmed ledge melted into his back and he dozed off.

Pete shook Justin's shoulder. "Time to head back. We're running a little late. I'm a sucker for a warm afternoon at the quarry, but I have another group to take out later for a sunset kayak."

Justin opened his eyes and looked up at the clouds that drifted across the sky. This time, when he got into the kayak, he easily paddled back out of the narrow channel to open water. He rolled his shoulders and settled into a comfortable rhythm. He didn't mind that Pete and Blake were ahead of him. He looked to see if he could spot the seals again.

As they paddled around the islands, a strong wind began to blow. Choppy waves churned up around them. When they neared the channel where the monster boat had rocked them, the sun disappeared behind the clouds. Waves pushed back on their kayaks, and Justin had to pull harder on his paddle to stay on course.

"We'd better make tracks," Pete called back over his shoulder as his kayak sliced through the waves. Off to their left, dark gray clouds piled up in the sky like dirty mounds of snow.

Then he heard the roar of an engine behind him, a large speedboat coming fast. Too fast. Justin dipped his paddle in, out, in, out. His tired muscles ached. In, out, in, out.

Without further warning, the boat zoomed past them and slued sharply toward the channel. Justin's kayak rocked violently from side to side. Justin gasped. Roll gently from your hips, he told himself.

"Watch out for that boat!" Pete yelled as the power boat skimmed close to his kayak. He dipped his paddle in the water to keep the kayak steady, as it rocked back and forth.

"Pete, you all right?" Blake shouted. Justin turned to see Pete's kayak roll sideways between the wake of the speedboat and the waves churned up by the wind. Blake paddled toward Pete.

The speedboat careened in a circle and headed toward shore. Justin's eyes widened as a person flew out of the boat and into the water. A head went under and bobbed back up again. The speedboat drove straight into rocks by the shoreline. Crash! Hung up on the rocks, it swung back and forth.

The boy was Tim, the speedster Pete had yelled at. His head sank under the water and bobbed up again. Justin hesitated. "Hang on! Tread water!" he yelled, hoping the boy could hear him. In, out, in, out. Pains shot through Justin's shoulders as he paddled toward the boy in the water. He thought the kid looked probably no more than twelve years old. What was he doing out here driving a boat on his own? "Stay calm. Don't thrash around." Justin called and paddled closer. "Move your feet gently to keep you afloat."

"I'm gonna drown!"

"No, you're not. Just hang on."

"But it's so cold."

"You're going to be okay."

Tim's arms flailed about, churning the water around him. His head sank under the water and bobbed up again.

"Keep calm." Justin looked at his paddle. If he stuck that out for Tim to grab onto, Tim would probably pull over the kayak and Justin would be stuck upside down. Cautiously, he leaned over and unhooked the skirt that confined him in the kayak. He had on a life vest, so even though the skirt was heavy, he would float. Rocking the kayak gently, he slipped over the side. "Yikes!" The coldness of the water shocked him for a moment. Struggling with the cumbersome skirt, he held on to the kayak and kicked his feet as he pushed the kayak towards Tim.

"Relax! Grab onto the kayak." Justin maneuvered the kayak with one hand and reached out to grab hold of Tim. Water splashed him in the face, but he had hold of Tim's shirt and hauled him toward the kayak. Finally, Tim stopped flailing and grabbed the kayak.

"Okay. Hang on and don't let go. We're going to hang onto the kayak until we get to shore." Justin began kicking his legs and the kayak moved toward shore. "Kick your legs, and we'll get there faster." Tim coughed up water, but began to kick.

When they had nearly reached the shoreline, Pete and Blake drifted up near them. Pete's paddle was stretched from his kayak to Blake's. He held on with one arm while the other arm hung limply at his side. Blake was paddling to keep both kayaks moving.

You okay?" Blake called.

"Yeah." Justin kept kicking. He was exhausted but wouldn't give up.

Blake and Pete reached shore first. One at a time, Pete pulled in the kayaks with one hand. Blake jumped out and swam out to Justin and Tim. He grabbed the kayak and helped pull it to shore. He pried Tim's hands off the kayak and dragged him onto the beach. Tim's teeth were chattering. Blake pulled the extra sweatshirts out of the hatches of the kayaks and helped Justin and Tim into them.

Justin watched as Pete set off a couple of flares that he kept in his kayak. Pete held his arm tightly by his side.

"What's wrong with your arm? Is it broken?"

"Nah, I don't think so, but it hurts like a son of a gun. Something flew out of that crazy boat and hit me in the arm."

The four of them huddled together to keep warm. A few minutes later, a passing speedboat pulled in. "Saw your flare. Need some help?"

"Yeah," said Pete. "Can we get a ride?"

"Sure thing. Looks like some kind of accident out there." The boat's captain looked at the wreckage of the speedboat stuck on a rock along the shore of the island. "What happened?"

"An accident," said Pete. "Can you take us back to the harbor? I'll send someone back for the kayaks."

The four of them waded out to the boat. No one said anything as the boat sped back toward the mainland. When the boat was moored, Tim smiled weakly at Justin. "Thanks. You saved my life. I'm sorry about what happened." He looked away and Justin could see tears in his eyes.

Justin nodded. He gritted his teeth, angry at the danger Tim had caused.

Tim went into the Kayak Rental Cabin to call his parents. Pete shook hands with Justin and Blake. "Thanks, guys. I'm sorry your kayaking trip turned out like this."

"It was an adventure I won't forget," Justin said. "What'll happen to Tim?"

"Hopefully, he won't be out in a boat alone until he's old enough and smart enough to know how to handle it. I'll be talking to his parents. Tim and his parents may be in a spot of trouble."

"What about your arm? Don't you need to see a doctor?"

"I'll get a ride back to town and check it out after I make arrangements to pick up those kayaks." Pete didn't look too happy. He headed off to the kayak rental office.

"Hey," Blake said. "Looks like you know something about lifesaving."

"Yeah, I took lifesaving at the Y. I guess that part stuck with me."

"Good thing your parents let you stay here while they were away. Maybe you can teach me about that lifesaving. Could come in handy."

"Trade you for diving lessons."

"Deal. You go in and get warm. I'll call my dad to come get us."

FUN FACTS:

What is a sea kayak?

Sea kayaks are usually longer than kayaks used on inland lakes or rivers. They have pedals that you can use to help steer the kayak. The "skirts" are vinyl, and after you put them on, they are clipped to the cockpit of the kayak. They keep you dry while paddling in the ocean.

How are sea otters different from river otters?

Sea otters are larger than river otters. They float on their backs, while river otters swim on their belies like muskrats. The sea otter's tail is short and flattened, while a river otter's tail is long and pointed. River otters can swim in the ocean as well as in rivers.

(oceanconservancy.org/blog/2019/01/30/tell-difference-sea-otters-river-otters/)

Mystery at the French Cathedral

Avery's foot kicked a silver pail full of dark red roses as she followed her mom across the plaza of the Hotel de Ville. When the pail started to tip over, she grabbed it and set it upright. "Pardon," she muttered to the flower seller, who shook a finger at her.

"C'est jolie." Avery's mom stopped to smell tall, fuchsia carnations in a metal can. "Perhaps we should buy some and take them back to our hotel room."

"Sure, I guess." Avery watched a group of French students, who sipped cups of steaming coffee at a table in an outdoor café. "Let's stop at that café."

"No time right now. Your dad and brother have gotten ahead of us again." She gestured toward the man and boy ahead who turned left down a narrow, brick-paved street.

"Why do we have to visit all of the cathedrals?" Avery shook her head.

"We went to the art museum yesterday to see the Cézanne paintings, so today it's cathedrals." Her mother patted her arm.

"That's true. It was great to see the Cézanne paintings that my art teacher talks about so much."

Avery and her mom followed the same narrow street and stopped in front of a massive stone cathedral. Her brother Drew looked up at the carved angel standing at the peak above the door while their dad read aloud from a guidebook. "The spiked spire on the right is said to have been a signal to the Knights Templar."

Avery looked up at the stone figures that stood in every crevice along the stone arch above the doors. Each one was carved of a different figure. Saints, maybe?

"Hey, the Knights Templar used to meet here. It says they fought in the Crusades. I'll bet there are tunnels and all kinds of secret hiding places in there." Drew pulled open the heavy wooden door and stepped inside.

Avery watched two French girls who sat on a bench across the narrow street, talking to two boys who stood in front of them. When she turned back to the Cathedral, the rest of her family was no longer beside her.

She opened the door and stepped into the dim, quiet entryway. To her right was a gift shop with wrought iron racks of postcards, candles, and rosaries. Wooden construction beams and a collection of tools lay scattered on the floor of a side chapel.

Drew watched a man walk across the scaffolding that stretched along one wall. To a ten-year-old, everything seemed fascinating, Avery thought. Two years ago, when she was ten, she didn't think she had been quite so dorky.

Avery turned left and walked into the main part of the cathedral. Coolness settled around her, a relief from the heat outside. Flames from rows of white votive candles cast flickering shadows across the stone walls.

There were only a few people inside the cathedral. Probably other people's families didn't visit every cathedral in France on their vacations, Avery thought. They probably had other, more fun things to do.

In the back pew, two elderly women dressed in black with black lace scarves on their heads silently moved their mouths as they fingered rosary beads. A family with two small children lit a candle in a side chapel.

Avery stopped to admire a large, golden cherub holding a candelabra. If that was real gold, it would be worth a fortune. She read the plaque beside it. "This candelabra was found in a secret vault only fifty years ago when the Cathedral was undergoing renovations. It was believed to date back to the twelfth century."

She wandered toward the front of the cathedral. Her parents stood at the altar, a slab of brown marble on top of a twisted tubular gold pedestal. Her dad read from the brochure that he held in his hand, "… and the exquisite tubular base was cast by the well-known metal artist…"

Not stopping to find out who the artist was, she walked past the altar. On the other side of the cathedral, she gazed up at the heavy stone beams holding up the ceiling. From the corner of her eye, she saw something move across from where she stood. She turned to stare at the cherub candelabra. It appeared to be slowly sliding backward across the wooden pedestal. No, that couldn't be. She rubbed her eyes and looked again. Now it wasn't there at all! Where did it go?

She walked over to the table where the candelabra had stood. And then she saw him. A man wearing gray pants and a huge gray coat with his arms held across the front of his body crept soundlessly toward a side door. Without thinking, Avery followed him around the corner. She halted when another man, tall and slender with very black hair, held the door open for him. He turned and looked straight into her eyes, as the other man stepped through the door and quietly shut it.

Avery hurried to the door and turned the knob. The door was locked. She read the sign that said, "Privé." Private, huh?

That man looked so suspicious. Was this a robbery in progress? She hadn't imagined it, had she? She turned around. Her mom stood in the gift shop, pulling postcards from the rack. Avery hurried across the cathedral.

"Mom," she whispered. "Did you see that golden cherub candelabra?"

"Uh-huh. Pretty, isn't it?"

"Well, now it isn't there." Avery looked at her mom, but her mom was looking at the two postcards in her hand.

"Which one of these do you think shows the Cathedral the best? This one that shows all of it from a distance, or this one that shows part of it up close?'

Avery sighed. "Both are fine."

Avery abandoned her mom and looked around for a guard. She spotted a man in a gray uniform who was standing by the museum entrance.

"Parlez-vous anglais?" She hoped he spoke English because that would be so much easier.

"Non."

"Le porte." Avery pointed at the side door. "Il est privé?"

"C'est pour les Sœurs de la Madeleine. Pas pour les touristes."

Avery felt a little insulted when he said it wasn't for tourists, but at least she knew now what the door opened into. But if it was for the nuns of Magdalene, what were those men doing in there? Perhaps she was imagining things. After all, who would steal something right in the open like that?

"Your dad and Drew are going to do a little shopping. Let's you and I stop at the plaza café on our way." Avery's mom touched her arm and strolled toward the cathedral doors. Avery eagerly followed her. At last, they could do something French, not act like tourists.

They squeezed into two chairs by a small round table in the crowded café. Avery looked around at all the stylish French people. A young man strode up to their table. "Quest-ce que vous voulez?"

"Pour mois, je voudrais un café." Avery's mom smiled as she tried out her French when she ordered a coffee.

"And pour vous, Mademoiselle. You would like what?" Avery looked up, and he was smiling at her. He had curly brown hair and brown eyes, and he looked just a little older than her. He was lucky to have a job in a café instead of vacationing with his family.

"Do you speak English?"

"Oui, Mademoiselle. Yes. I practice the English on the Americans."

"Vous parlez bien. I am practicing my French on the French." They both laughed. "Une chocolate chaud, s'il vous plait."

He bowed and walked away with their order. When he returned, he placed two napkins and their drinks on the table.

"A café and a hot chocolate. You would like anything else?"

"Non, merci. Quel est votre nom?" Avery's mom gave him a bright smile.

"My name, it is Michel. My father, he owns the café. Me, I am, how do you say? I am stuck here waiting on the tables all day. You are on vacation, n'est-ce pas?'

"C'est vrais. We are the tourists, I'm sorry to say."

Michel laughed. "You are on the vacation in Aix-en-Provence and wish to be doing something else. I am at home and wish to be on the vacation anywhere."

Avery laughed. "Perhaps we should trade places."

"But you have seen the Cézannes, n'est-ce pas? Cézanne, he is very famous here."

Oh, oui. We loved the Cézanne paintings of the mountains."

The rest of the day included lunch in an outdoor café, a visit to another cathedral across town, looking at one pottery shop after another, and eating pastries in a patisserie. Avery did not have time to think about the two men she had seen taking the candelabra.

When her parents ran out of energy, they all went back to the hotel to rest before dinner. Her mom asked the young man at the desk for their keys, and they climbed the wide staircase to the second floor. Avery noticed again how small the doors seemed that lined the narrow, carpeted hallway. She could see how this used to be a convent.

Her mom inserted the key into the door to the room at the end of the hall. "For dinner, let's try that cute little restaurant by the Hotel de Ville. I'll bet they have interesting French food."

"I'm ready for a nap," her dad said.

Avery entered her room across the hall from their parents. Drew unlocked the door to his room next to hers, grabbed his game box out of his backpack, and knocked on Avery's door.

Avery knew it would be Drew. They each wanted their own rooms, but Drew didn't usually want to be alone in his room unless it was bedtime.

"Come in." Avery continued to look at her phone. One text from a friend from home.

Drew entered the room, sat in the chair by the bed and began to play a game. Avery knew he wouldn't be a pest and would leave if she asked him to go to his own room. Some-times they both wanted the company.

Avery opened the wooden shutters and looked out the second story window at the courtyard below. It was empty, except for a few round tables with chairs and a couple of large urns with colorful flowers. Next door to the hotel, she could see people sitting at tables arranged around a fountain at an outdoor café. The whine of accordion music drifted upward. Suddenly, she gasped and quickly closed the shutters.

Drew looked up. "What's wrong with you? You look like you saw a ghost or something."

"It's him." Avery's eyes grew wider.

"Who?"

"The tall man who saw me at the Cathedral. He's sitting in the café next to the hotel."

"What man?"

"Do you remember that cupid candelabra? The one that was about this high and all gold?"

"You mean the one they found in the vault? I'll bet the Knights Templar put it there."

"Yes, that one. A man in a dark coat picked it up and hid it underneath his coat. Then a tall man opened the door marked "private" and they left with it."

"Wow. Do you really think that man stole that candle thing right in front of everyone?"

"I don't know. There wasn't anyone else around. No one saw him except me. But they looked suspicious."

"But if they went through a private door, maybe they just work at the Cathedral and were moving it somewhere else."

"They looked like they were up to something. And the tall man looked right at me as he left, glaring at me, like he was warning me. It made me shiver."

"Did you tell anyone?"

"Mom didn't seem to think anything of it."

"You know Mom when she's doing her tourist thing. Let me see what he looks like." Drew opened the shutters and stuck his head out the window.

"Don't let him see you. He's sitting by himself at that corner table."

Drew looked down into the café. "There's a couple at one table and a family with a baby at another. I don't see anyone else."

Avery looked again, but the man was no longer sitting at the table. "Maybe that means he lives near here. What if he's staying right here at this hotel?"

"Don't worry about it." Drew went back to his game.

Avery paced around the room and then flopped on the bed and stared at the ceiling.

An hour later, their dad knocked on the door. "Fifteen minutes to dinner."

Avery and her family walked through the narrow streets. The sun was going down as people lowered large wooden or metal doors over their shops. People hurried home at the end of the day, while tourists ambled down the streets and stopped to read menus in the restaurant windows.

Avery's dad read the map while her mom looked at the street signs to direct them to the restaurant. The narrow streets seemed to diverge in all directions. Avery tried to remember which way they had come from the hotel. She kept looking over her shoulder, but didn't see the tall man behind them.

At the plaza of the Hotel de Ville, they entered a small restaurant with only a few tables. A nice-looking man hurried to greet them with a smile. "Monsieurs, Madame, Mademoiselle. Bon soir." He showed them to a table by the window.

Avery looked around at the artwork on the walls that someone had created using kitchen utensils. On one wall, a wreath of spoons was decorated with red ribbons. On another a saucepan had a face drawn on it with scouring pads for hair.

She studied the menu and tried to find something that looked familiar.

"What's calmar?" Drew frowned at the menu.

Avery's dad thumbed through his French-English dictionary. "Squid."

"Cool. I'll have that."

"Gross." Avery made a face. "I think I'll have the salade nicoise and vicchysoise." There couldn't be anything weird in a salad or potato soup.

Avery took a piece of bread from the basket and bit into it. The outside crust had a satisfying crunch, and the inside was soft and delicious. She looked around at the other people in the restaurant. A French couple sat at the table beside them, looking into each other's eyes. At a table by the wall sat a family with two small children.

When the salade nicoise arrived, Avery poked suspiciously at something gray and slippery on top. "What's that?"

"Looks like anchovies." Her mom smiled. "Salade nicoise always has anchovies."

"Now you tell me."

"Give them to me. I'll eat them." Her dad forked them off her plate and onto his.

Avery inspected the soup, but didn't find anything she didn't recognize. She finished her soup and salad and ordered chocolate mouse for dessert. When she had finished the last bite, she gazed out the window into the darkened streets, while the rest of her family finished eating. Suddenly, she slouched down in her seat and looked away. There he was again, the tall man, walking with the stocky man wearing a dark coat and brimmed hat.

She turned to her mom, who was sipping espresso. "Drew and I are really tired. I guess we'll go back to the hotel and wait for you there."

"I'm not tired."

Avery kicked him under the table.

"Ow!" Drew scowled at her.

"Sorry, it was an accident."

"Go with your sister. Here, take the map." Dad pulled a map out of his pocket and handed it to Drew.

"Do I have to?" Drew grumbled. Avery pulled on his arm, and reluctantly he stood up. She hurried him out the door.

"Why do we have to go back to the hotel?"

"It's the tall man. He just walked by. We have to follow him. I'll bet he'll lead us to the cherub candelabra."

"Are you crazy? Then what are we going to do?"

"Tell the cops."

"How are you going to find one?"

"Come on." Avery looked down the street. The two men walked quickly, already a block ahead. "Hurry."

Light from inside the restaurants and cafés bathed the street in pale gold. It was empty of pedestrians, and Avery's shoes clicked loudly in the quiet. When the tall man stopped to light a cigarette, Avery pulled Drew into a doorway and waited before peering around the corner.

"They're headed toward the Cathedral! I'll bet they hid the candelabra right there because no one would suspect it."

In the Plaza of the Hotel de Ville, streetlamps flung shadows across the cobblestones. During the day it had been filled with people and flowers and sunshine. Now a small group of men who stood at the corner watched them pass, and Avery and Drew walked closer together.

As they turned into the side street that led to the Cathedral, they saw the two men already going inside. They ran to the door and Avery opened it slowly. She silently thanked someone for keeping the hinges oiled, so the door didn't creak. They tiptoed in and peered into the apse of the cathedral.

The door marked "Privé" was ajar. They edged toward it and peered around the door frame. Inside was a courtyard outlined with columns. A fountain sat in the center, surrounded by low bushes and pots of flowers. On the far side, they saw the tall man lift something out of a large urn. Gold gleamed in the faint light just before he put it into a large bag.

Drew gasped, and just then the tall man started to turn around. Drew ducked back behind the door. He grabbed Avery's arm and pulled her toward him. Avery was sure they wouldn't be able to open the heavy door and leave before the tall man reached them. She ducked into a side chapel, and together they huddled beneath a bench. The door opened and closed, and then opened and closed again. Did that mean both men had left? Soft footsteps crept toward the chapel where they hid. Avery put her hand over her mouth to quiet her breathing. After the footsteps slowly passed, Avery peered around the bench. She nudged Drew. They slipped off their shoes and tiptoed toward the door as they heard voices from the half-open door marked Privé.

"There's no one here. It's late, and the Cathedral is usually locked."

"But I thought I heard someone breathing."

"Pull yourself together. You're imagining things. Never mind. Help me with this."

Avery and Drew opened the heavy door and tore down the street toward the Plaza. As they rounded the corner, Avery looked over her shoulder. Suddenly, she slammed into a body in front of her and screamed.

"Pardon, pardon, mademoiselle. Please do not scream." The young voice sounded alarmed, and Avery looked up at Michel from the café.

"Oh, Michel, they're after us." She looked around and quickly tugged him into an arched doorway.

Drew crowded in behind them. He pointed at Michel. "Who's that?"

"Shh." Avery pulled Drew in closer. "It's Michel"

"Who…" Drew started, but Avery shook her head

"Quest-ce que ce? What is the problem?" Michel whispered.

Avery told him in whispers about the Cathedral and the candelabra.

"Do you think this can be so?" Michel frowned.

"Oui. I am sure. You do not believe me?"

Michel shrugged. "If you say it is so, it must be so." He looked at Drew. "And you also saw this happen?"

"No, I didn't see anything, except that one minute the candelabra was there, and then it wasn't."

"Will you come with us to the police?" Avery touched Michel's arm.

Michel frowned again.

"S'il vous plait. C'est important. Please. It's important."

"We could solve the mystery of the theft and be heroes." Drew nodded.

Michel shrugged. "D'accord." They peered out and looked right and left. They did not see anyone following them. They stepped out into the street and hurried to the Prefecture de Police across from the café that Michel's family owned.

Michel conversed with the police officers, and Avery did her best to look serious and concerned. She understood part of what Michel said and nodded her encouragement.

Finally, the policeman shrugged. "Bon. I will go just to make you happy, but you must go home to your papa." He turned to Avery and Drew. "This policeman will escort you to the hotel. We do not want young Americans wandering around in the dark."

Reluctantly, Avery and Drew walked with the policeman back to their hotel. As they retrieved the key from the concierge and walked up the steps, their parents arrived downstairs. They raced quietly down the hall and into their room.

"But now we'll never know what happened." Avery stared out the window, wishing their room looked out on the Cathedral.

Drew shrugged. "We probably imagined the whole thing."

"No, we didn't."

"Don't worry. We'll find out tomorrow. We can always go back to the café and talk to Michel."

"True." Avery smiled at the thought of talking to Michel again. "Better go to your room and get ready for bed, I guess."

"Goodnight."

"Goodnight. Sleep loose."

After their parents stopped in to say goodnight, Avery sat on her bed for a long time and thought about the two men and the candelabra. Had they really been thieves? Or was she just imagining it because she wanted to solve a mystery?

The next morning while they were eating breakfast, a young policeman came into the breakfast room with Michel right behind him. He looked around the room, and Michel gestured to where the family was sitting. They walked up to the table.

"Bonjour, monsieur, madame." The policeman nodded to Avery's parents. Michel smiled at Avery.

"Mademoiselle, you were correct. The candelabra, it was stolen. But we have found it. You described very well how the thieves looked. They did not get far. And we wish to thank you and your brother."

"Merci for believing us. I'm glad you caught the thieves." Avery smiled.

"Hey, you found them! Tres bon. Good." Drew grinned.

The policeman nodded to them both. "Merci, merci. We are grateful for your help." He bowed and then turned and walked briskly out of the hotel.

"What is going on?" Dad frowned and raised his eyebrows.

"What candelabra?" Mom looked at Avery and then at Drew.

"Mom," said Avery, "you remember Michel from the café. Where we had coffee and chocolate."

Mom smiled at Michel. "Of course. Sit down, avez-vous une café." Mom gestured to an empty chair, and Michel sat next to Avery.

"Please explain," said Dad.

Avery began to explain how on the visit to the Cathedral she had seen the candelabra disappear. How later she had seen the thieves, and she and Drew had followed them back to the Cathedral. She was grateful that Michel helped explain what happened next. Her parents listened without yelling. Later, they might have more to say about it.

"We will talk more later about dangerous situations and keeping safe." Dad gave Avery and Drew a serious look, then sipped his coffee.

"I go to the café. We are open for le petit-dejeuner, the breakfast."

Drew shook Michel's hand. "Merci for your help."

Michel rose to leave, and Avery walked with him outside the hotel.

"Merci." Avery looked at Michel. "Good thing we ran into you."

"You have an adventure on your vacance, n'est-ce pas? So, it is not so boring." He smiled.

"Oui. This vacation was definitely an adventure. We leave tomorrow. I will come to the café to say goodbye." She smiled back.

"Bon. Au revoir. I will see you tomorrow." Michel strode through the gate and down the street.

FUN FACTS:

Where is Aix-en-Provence?

Aix-en-Provence is a university city in the Provence-Alpes-Côte d'Azur region of southern France. The white limestone mountain of Sainte-Victoire overlooks the city.

(wikipedia.org/wiki/Aix-en-Provence)

Who was Paul Cézanne?

Paul Cézanne was born in Aix-en-Provence and often painted landscapes of the mountains, Mont Sainte-Victoire. He adopted many ideas about modern art from the Impressionists. Cézanne is now known as a Post-Impressionist, and is sometimes called the father of modern art. He encouraged artists to explore color, shape and space without needing to make sense in a realistic way.

(britannica.com/biography/Paul-Cezanne)

Atelihai (Hello or Welcome)

Kylie and Jaden sat at the kitchen table of the rental house in Anchorage, eating toast and scrambled eggs. Their moms sat in the living room with their grandma, looking at something on the computer. Their dads stood outside and looked at the mountains.

"What are they planning for today, do you think?" Jaden looked at Kylie.

"We're all going to the Botanical Gardens this morning, I think. My mom found one that we can walk to. Grandma said we all need a walk after the long flights yesterday."

"Oh, do you think we all have to go?"

"Sure, you'll love it. All those plants and flowers."

"Maybe. I think Dad wants to visit the Anchorage Museum this afternoon. He read that there are examples of the boats Indigenous people used that he wants to see. You know my dad and boats."

"True. Museums are usually cool. Since I was little, my parents have taken me to all kinds of them, everywhere we go."

Jaden laughed. "Mine, too."

At the botanical garden, their dads strolled on ahead. Their moms and grandparents stopped to look at every flower they saw along the trail.

"If we go this way, we'll meet up with them later on." Jaden pointed to the map of the gardens on the sign.

"Good plan."

"I didn't think Grandpa is that interested in flowers."

"Me either. I think he just wants to hang out with Grandma and his two daughters. You know, like it was on family vacations before we were even born."

"Guess so."

Jaden and Kylie walked off in a different direction. Their grandpa looked up and waved.

"So, cousin, how is sixth grade?" Jaden looked down at Kylie. She noticed how tall he had gotten.

"It's different. Some things are better. Like, we have more subjects than we did in elementary school. I got to take Spanish this year, and that's really cool."

"Yeah, I liked that part, too."

"Making friends is harder, because there are so many kids that I don't know who went to other elementary schools than I did. But in a way it's good, because there are new people to get to know."

"Friendships change a lot in middle school."

"How do you like eighth grade? Is it really hard?"

"The work is harder, but I like that the teachers don't treat us so much like little kids, and we're the oldest kids in the school, so the younger kids look up to us."

"Have you made a lot of friends?"

"Not a lot, but the friends I have are really tight. We look out for each other."

"I thought you might not come with all of us to Alaska."

"Why not? Who wouldn't want to visit Alaska? Anyway, Mom would never have let me stay home. She really wanted all of us and the grandparents to do something together."

"My mom did, too. Well, I'm glad you came."

"Glad you did, too. It'd be a bit slow with just the grownups."

Kylie laughed. "Look at those blue flowers. I love that color." She bent down and read the label, Hungarian Blue Breadseed Poppy. I wonder if Mom could grow these in our garden."

"Interesting name. Good color, though."

Their second day in Anchorage, they drove to the Alaska Native Heritage Center and watched a dance performance by Indigenous people. Afterward, they walked through the outdoor exhibits. They visited three types of houses used by Indigenous people, Athabascan, Yupik, and Ulax, who lived underground during the winter. Inside the houses, Indigenous guides described what life would have been like for the communities that lived there.

A large plank house displayed the totems of the different peoples and the mottos of the group: Eyak "Respect for Culture"; Tlingit, "Respect for Self"; Haida, "Respect for Family"; Timshian, "Respect for the environment."

"Look what the sign says." Kylie pointed to the wooden display sign. "Children inherit all their rights through their mothers."

"Sounds good," said their mothers together and laughed.

The next day, on their way to Seward on the Kenai Peninsula, they visited Exit Glacier and hiked to view it up close.

"The glacier has retreated a really long distance." Jaden pointed to the picture display sign by the trail. "This shows where the glacier was in 1815 with markers for years since, up until 2007. That's a long retreat."

"Climate change," said his dad.

From a distance, the glacier looked white, but when they got closer it looked blue.

"I've never seen a glacier," said Kylie. "How interesting to live somewhere there are glaciers you can visit anytime."

"How true," said Jaden.

Perched at the head of Resurrection Bay off the Gulf of Alaska, Seward was not very big. Everyone in the family exclaimed at the beauty of the snow-covered mountains that surrounded the town. After settling into their rental place, they drove to Kenai Fjords National Park. The ferry for their tour waited at the dock. It was large enough for 24 people, but only twelve had signed up for this tour. The eight family members chose two inside booths next to each other. Kylie and Jaden stood on the deck of the ferry, watching two sea otters swim near the shoreline in Seward Harbor.

"Look. They're swimming on their backs. I knew they did that, but never saw one for real." Kylie pointed to the sea otters.

"Me either. The pictures of them are always so cute. But they look smaller than I thought they would be."

"We are ready to shove off." They heard the captain's voice over the speaker. "You can see the sea otters off to the right of the boat, but we will not see much wildlife until we get farther out in the fjords."

Snow-covered mountains rose majestically on both sides of the fjord, as the boat passed by on its way to the open water.

"Hey, I got up once last night because I thought it was morning. When I looked out, I could still see the sun, but the clock said it was 2:00 a.m.!" Kylie looked at Jaden.

"Guess that's what they mean by the midnight sun. I slept so soundly that I missed it. I'll have to set my alarm, so I can get up to see that."

Soon they saw no more houses along the shore, and their boat was the only boat in sight. Large rocky formations stood in the water like small islands in the fjords. Golden-brown bodies lay among the rocks, and small brown heads bobbed in the water nearby.

"Off to your left, you can see Stellar sea lions by the grottos of the Inner Chiswell Islands." The pilot pointed toward the golden-brown bodies.

"Cool," said Kylie and took their picture.

"Farther along you can see the homes of the puffins who also enjoy the rocky islands." The pilot slowed the boat as they passed the many birds sitting on or flying around the rocky islands.

The boat turned right and drove toward a blue-ice glacier. "This is another tidal glacier, named the Northwest Glacier. Watch for a few minutes and see if the glacier calves, meaning a piece of it will fall off."

Everyone stood at the railing and watched. Time passed, but suddenly, there it was. "There it goes!" someone yelled as the piece of the glacier plopped into the water.

The boat slowly drove along the shore. Small bergs floated in the water, just big enough for two seals to lie on them. A couple of seals looked up at the boat as it passed, but most of them slept on. Kylie took a picture of one who watched them as they glided by.

"It's amazing that there are no other boats in sight, just us," said Jaden.

The boat moved on, and the pilot pointed out other tidal glaciers. Suddenly, whales began popping up all around them.

"Wow! Look!" The whales popped up like popcorn in a popcorn popper. Kylie focused her camera and waited until the next one surfaced to snap a photo.

"These are humpback whales and are most likely feeding, having found a plentiful source of food." Two whales surfaced at once near the boat, and everyone on the boat cheered.

"We have to get to Homer today," Grandpa announced while eating breakfast. "Halibut capital of the world, you know."

"Fresh halibut sounds good," said Kylie's dad.

On the drive around to the other side of the peninsula to visit Homer, they stopped at an historic restaurant in Kenai for lunch and checked out the nearby beach.

"Definitely too cold for swimming," said Jaden's mom.

Homer was a small town which included a long, narrow spit of land reaching out into the ocean. Just one road ran down the middle of it. Jaden's dad parked the car, and they walked down the narrow road. Small shops, art galleries, and seafood restaurants crowded both sides. Outside the restaurant where they ate dinner, Kylie took a picture of her grandpa in front of a life-size wooden halibut and fisherman. He looked at the camera with a wide grin on his face

The following day they drove back to Anchorage to return the rental car, and fly to Juneau.

"Look, isn't that a moose?" Jaden pointed to the side of the road that led to the airport.

"And a baby moose. Cute," Kylie said.

"I didn't expect to see a moose so close to town," said Grandpa.

"Let's stop, so we can take a picture," said Grandma.

"Okay, but we'd better keep our distance, so we don't disturb them," said Kylie's dad.

In Juneau, they rented another van and drove into town. Two cruise ships were docked in the port, and tourists crowded the street. In the park on the edge of town they stopped to watch a drum circle, part of a celebration by the Sealaska Native Institute.

The next morning at the bed and breakfast, their hostess explained how to get to Mendenhall Glacier.

"Turn right from the front of the house and walk out to the main road. Turn right again and keep walking. It's only about a mile, an easy walk."

"Great. I could use a walk," said Grandma.

Walking with their parents and grandparents on the way to Mendenhall Glacier National Park seemed to take a long time. Their mothers and grandparents seldom saw each other all together, so there was a lot of talking. Once in a while the whole group would stop and gesture to the view of the snow-covered mountains or the wildflowers that grew along the sidewalk. A lot of talk about remembering past vacations. "Remember when we went on that vacation to Lake Superior,

The Dells, and so on." Kylie and Jaden looked at each other and rolled their eyes.

Finally, they reached the entrance to the park and saw the glacier up ahead.

"It looks a lot like Exit Glacier," Kylie said. She gazed at the blue ice that flowed between the mountains down into the lake. Snow-covered mountains rose up behind it, with a water fall tumbling down the mountain on one side.

"Hand me your camera. I'll take your picture in front of the glacier." Jaden held out his hand. He took Kylie's picture, and then the family had to have pictures of all the possible combinations. Kylie and Jaden. Jaden with his parents and Kylie with her parents. The grandparents. Finally, Kylie's mother asked a young woman walking by if she would take a picture of all of them together.

"Whew," said Jaden. "Glad the picture-taking is over. Let's take the Glacier Trail."

"I don't know, Jaden. It might be too much for your grandmother." His mother said to him in a quiet voice.

"That's okay. Let the kids walk that one. Grandpa and I will watch the video at the Visitor Center and then look around. It's a beautiful day, so we can sit and watch the water-fall until you get back."

Jaden and Kylie set off walking. Their dads followed, while their mothers decided to stay with the grandparents.

The trail led through lush greenery of trees and bushes. They crossed a stream on a wooden bridge and looked down at a waterfall. Along the trail they glimpsed the glacier through gaps in the trees. And then suddenly they were close to it. When they returned to the Visitor Center, the rest of the family was sitting on a bench waiting for them.

"We'll take our time walking back," said Kylie's mom. She nodded to Kylie and Jaden. "You two can go on ahead, if you like. We'll catch up to you."

"Okay," said Jaden. "We'll see you in a few." Jaden and Kylie walked along the sidewalk. A couple of cars passed by them going toward Mendenhall Glacier, but the road was mostly quiet.

Suddenly, Kylie's eyes opened wider. Why had someone placed a sculpture of a black bear right beside the sidewalk like that? Then the sculpture turned its head slowly and looked right at her. She took a quick breath. That is not a sculpture! That is a real bear!

She grabbed Jaden's arm and whispered, "There's a bear on the left just a few feet ahead of us."

Jaden looked to his left and stopped suddenly. Without saying anything, Jaden grabbed her arm and the two of them began to back up slowly.

"What if it follows us?" Kylie whispered again.

"Let's hope it doesn't."

The bear did not come any closer. It watched them from the middle of the road. And then it turned and walked across the road into the woods on the other side.

"Wow! That was unexpected!" Kylie let out her breath.

"You can say that again!" Jaden shook his head. "I've never met a bear up close like that."

"Me either." Kylie paused. "That was pretty amazing, though."

"Yeah, it was. This vacation has been amazing, but I think I will always remember this part the best."

"Me, too. The bear looked right at me. He seemed so friendly and unconcerned about us."

"Good thing."

FUN FACTS:

Why is Exit Glacier named Exit Glacier?

Exit Glacier is one of five glaciers in the Harding Ice Field of the Kenai Mountains. In 1968 the first documented expedition crossed the ice field. The mountaineering party exited it by descending this particular glacier. And it became known as Exit Glacier.

(wikipedia.org/wiki/Exit_Glacier)

What should you do if you meet a black bear in the woods?

Black bears are usually shy around people and avoid them. If you see one, give it plenty of space. Back away slowly, don't run. Look large and talk calmly. Don't scream,

(nps.gov/subjects/bears/safety.htm)

What does Atelihai mean?

Atelihai, pronounced ahh-tee-lee-hi, is the Inuktitut word for "hello" or "welcome."

Family Vacation Deluxe

With two hands, Austin heaved his duffle bag into the SUV, climbed into the back seat, and sat by the window. His sister Peyton opened the door on the other side and sat by the opposite window.

"Hey, don't take up the whole back seat." His brother Aiden climbed in and nudged him over into the middle next to Peyton. It seemed like Aiden was growing so fast that he got larger every day. Austin wondered when he would start growing as fast as that.

"I was here first. I don't want to sit in the middle." Austin frowned at Aiden and tried to jostle him over.

"You're the smallest. I'm two years older than you and a lot bigger. You have to sit in the middle. We can trade later on."

"Well, I'm the oldest, so don't take up so much room." Peyton frowned at Aiden and gently nudged Austin over.

"But I'll get sick if I don't sit by the window." Austin felt tears in his eyes.

"If you feel sick, I'll open the window, or we can trade places later." Peyton patted Austen's shoulder. "Why do we always have to take a family vacation? I'm going to miss Melissa's birthday party and everyone else will be there."

Mom and Dad packed the last of the camping gear into the back and got into the front seat. "Everyone set? Off we go." Mom leaned back in her seat.

"Ready to roll." Dad whistled the beginning of "Take me out to the ballgame" as he backed the car out of the driveway. "Maine, here we come. I can't wait to taste that Maine lobster."

"Ew," said Peyton and Austin.

"Or those delicious Maine shrimp, said Mom.

"The shrimp aren't bad," said Aiden.

"It will be nice to see your grandparents again. We haven't seen them since last summer."

"I miss them," said Austin.

At the entrance to the freeway, Aiden groaned. "Looks like the entrance ramp is backed up. Is everyone going on vacation? I'm going to miss soccer practice and the big game this week. Why do families take vacations anyway?"

"Guess we'll have to creep along. We'll get out of town eventually." Dad continued to whistle. "And then we'll be off on a big adventure. It'll be loads of fun." He tapped his fingers on the steering wheel and moved the car a few inches at a time as the cars ahead crept along.

"Yeah, loads of fun," muttered Aiden.

"We should have just stayed home." Peyton slumped in her seat and closed her eyes.

"Let's play an alphabet game." Austin looked up at Peyton.

"Not right now. Maybe later." Peyton put on her headphones and turned toward the window.

Austin sighed, pulled two superheroes out of his pocket, and pretended they were saving someone from danger.

When their car reached the freeway entrance, a car slowed to let them merge. Traffic finally picked up speed, and the van lurched forward, Austin scrunched down in the seat, hoping his stomach wouldn't do flip-flops as it usually did when he rode in the van. Dad merged the car onto the highway, and the speed eased the flip-flops in his stomach.

"Want to name all the superheroes you can think of?" Austin nudged Aiden.

"Nah. I'm busy." Aiden pulled out his phone and brought up a video game.

"We're in good old Ohio," Dad called out. "Look at that impressive bridge over the river."

"Cool," said Austin.

A couple of hours later, Dad took an exit to a drive-through and pulled into the line to place an order. He whistled under his breath while he waited for the order to be ready. He took the order and pulled over into a parking spot. Taking out one item at a time, he handed them each a kid's meal. He handed Mom both of their orders and pulled the car back onto the highway. Mom handed him one item of food at a time, and he ate while he drove.

"A kid's meal?" Peyton looked at it in disgust. She nibbled at the chicken nuggets that used to be her favorite but no longer were, and tried a couple of fries. The soda was at least cold and refreshing.

"What toy did I get?" Austin quickly pulled out his toy. "I've already got this one. What did you get, Aiden?"

Aiden chewed quickly and had almost finished his burger. Still eating, he stuck his hand in the bag and pulled out his toy. He held it up for Austin to see.

"Hey, I don't have that one," said Austin. He looked at Peyton's toy. "Hey, I don't have that one either. Do you want to trade?"

"Here." Peyton handed Austin the toy she had gotten. "Keep them both."

"Have mine, too." Aiden handed him the toy.

"Hey, thanks." At least one of the toys was different from the ones he had. And it never hurt to have two of the same one. Austin put both toys in his pocket. He ate part of his burger and stuffed it back into the bag. "Mom, I don't feel so good."

"Just close your eyes and take deep breaths." Mom turned around and smiled encouragingly. "I'll turn up the fan, so you get more air." She turned the switch and settled back into her seat.

"Stop leaning against me." Peyton shrugged her shoulders and Austin sat up.

Austin tried to look out the window, but he couldn't see very well around Aiden or Peyton. "I think I'm going to be sick."

"Just take deep breaths," said Dad.

Austin breathed several times. "I think I'm going to be sick."

"You'd better stop," said Mom. "Remember what happened last time?"

"We'll pull off at the next exit," said Dad.

"I think I'm going to be sick now." Austin put his hand over his mouth.

Dad pulled the van to a sudden stop on the side of the highway.

"Watch it," Peyton moved out of the way as Austin climbed over her to get to the door. Just as Mom opened the door, Austin began to throw up.

"Ew." Peyton made a face and turned away.

Mom led him over to the grass and wiped his mouth with a tissue. She walked him up and down by the road a few times. "Okay now?"

Austin nodded. She hugged him, and they climbed back into the van.

"Let Austin sit by the window for a while," said Mom.

Aiden frowned but slid over and made room. "Don't even think about getting sick again."

Austin didn't answer. He didn't try to get sick, it just happened. He closed his eyes. Sometimes that helped.

A couple of hours later, Dad pointed out the window. "Look at beautiful Lake Erie right by the road as we drive through Pennsylvania. We're almost to New York State."

"Yeah, the longest state in the country," grumbled Aiden.

"What about Florida all the way to the Keys? Or California from north to south?" Mom turned in her seat and smiled at him.

Austin closed his eyes again and fell asleep. He woke up to the sound of the slap, slap, slap of a tire.

"What's that?" said Mom.

"Sounds like a flat tire." Dad eased the van off the highway. "Everybody out."

"This is going to take forever. Do you know how to change a flat?" Aiden looked at the tire that was squashed onto the gravel.

Peyton sighed, moved away from the rest of the family, and checked her phone.

"Sure. You can help. Let's get this stuff out of the van, so we can find the tire iron and jack." Dad opened the back and began to unload.

Aiden tossed out Austin's duffle and a few other things from the back of the van.

"Hey, careful with that!" Austin ran over, picked up the duffle and set it on the grass.

"Let's just stand here away from the road while we watch them fix it." His mom put her arm around Austin and pulled him onto the grass. "Let's see who can count the most license plates from different states."

Austin nodded, but his heart wasn't in it. "I'm thirsty." Austin held up his empty water bottle.

"We'll stop at a rest area down the road after the tire is fixed and fill up our water bottles. But you can have a drink from mine." Mom ruffled Austin's hair and handed him the water bottle,

"I think I have to go to the bathroom."

"Can you just wait a while? Or I can take you back there into that field."

"I'll wait."

Dad fit the jack under the car and pumped until the tire came up off the road. Grunting, he unscrewed the wheel nuts and directed Aiden to help him pull off the tire. He fit on the spare, retightened the nuts, and let down the jack. "Okay, let's get this stuff back in."

Aiden helped his dad load everything back so it fit in, and everyone got back into the van.

Aiden let Austin sit by the window.

"Are we almost there?" said Austin.

"No, not yet," said Mom.

"When are we going to eat dinner?" said Aiden.

"Next town." Said Dad. "We're almost out of the great state of New York and into the Green Mountains of Vermont."

The sun was setting into the hills, when suddenly everything gleamed with whiteness. "Look at that snow! Who would have thought it would be snowing up here in the mountains in August?" Dad braked the van, testing the road.

"Cool," said Aiden. "Maybe we can go skiing."

"But I want to get a tan." Peyton frowned.

"The town is all dark. The power must be out." Mom pointed at the neon signs that stood like bare trees along the road. "We were planning to stay here tonight."

"Guess we'll have to drive on. Looks like nothing is open." Dad began to whistle "White Christmas."

Aiden groaned. "I'm tired of riding."

"Where are we going to stop, then?" Peyton said.

Austin clutched his stomach and tried to breathe deeply.

"Hope we don't run out of gas," said Dad.

The next town was dark as well, and all the lights were out at the gas stations and motels. They drove on through the mountains, with not a motel in sight. Peyton and Aiden both fell asleep, leaning against Austin. Austin tried to push them away, but they were too heavy.

"There's one." Dad pulled the wheel to the left and drove into the driveway of an old motel. The partially lit up sign read, "-ountain -otel with the first letter in each word blacked out.

"I guess it'll have to do." Mom sighed and went into the motel with Dad. They came back and drove around to the side, where there were only two other cars parked.

"This is creepy," said Peyton. "There's no one else here."

"At least we've got a room," Dad said.

Inside, the room smelled like stale bread and dogs. "Yuk." Austin held his nose.

There were two double beds with brown comforters and a sagging couch. The matching lamps were red and gold, but only one of them came on when Mom flipped the switch.

"Looks like junkyard décor," said Peyton.

"What about dinner? I'm starved." Aiden looked out the window but didn't see a restaurant.

"Looks like crackers and cheese and a couple of shared apples." Mom pulled food out of a bag and began to pass it around.

"I'm not hungry." Austin sank down on one of the beds.

"Austin, eat a couple of crackers and get your shower. You look all done in." Mom handed him his pajamas and gently nudged him toward the bathroom.

Austin tried not to look at the moldy shower curtain as he turned on the water. He stepped into the shower and jumped as the cold water hit him. He quickly turned the hot water knob, but nothing happened. Shivering, he turned off the water and dried off with a towel that was as thin as paper.

"Where's everyone going to sleep?" Peyton glared at the double bed. It looked lumpy.

"I'll sleep on the couch." Dad pointed at the sagging couch with a blanket draped over the back. "I can sleep anywhere. Mom and Peyton will sleep in one bed, and Aiden and Austin in the other one. We'll manage."

"This is the only motel for miles around. We can't drive all night, so you'll just have to make the best of it. We're all tired, so just go to sleep." Mom's voice had that tone that even Peyton wouldn't question.

"This is the worst vacation yet." Peyton grabbed her pajamas and headed to the bathroom.

Austin didn't bother to tell her about the cold shower. He ignored the shriek from the bathroom as he climbed into bed and fell asleep.

In the morning, fog drifted around them and the wet air clung to their skin. "Where are we going to eat breakfast? I'm starving," Aiden said as they packed their things back into the van.

"We'll just have to keep driving until we find someplace." Dad began whistling the theme song from *The Wizard of Oz.*"

"I don't want to eat anyway." Peyton leaned her head against the window. "I'm too tired. Someone was snoring all night."

"It wasn't me." Austin didn't think that he snored, but if he did, it was because the motel was dusty and he had trouble breathing.

"Hey, look at that sign. We're in the beautiful Vermont mountains." Dad pointed to the sign.

"Beautiful." Mom looked out the window and smiled.

No one talked as they drove along a winding road that snaked through the mountains. Plenty of green pine trees dusted with snow lined the road, but there were no restaurants or gas stations.

Through the fog, Austin glimpsed twinkling, colored lights and a blinking sign. He pointed toward the lights. "Hey, how about that one?"

Up close, the brown log building looked like it had started in one direction and ended up in another. The words Dream Inn were painted in white on a small, blue sailboat. Out loud, Austin read the sign in the window, "Welcome. Eat and enjoy. Try our deluxe."

"It looks kind of run down," said Mom.

"Deluxe what?" Austin looked around at everybody, but no one answered.

"It's all we've got." said Dad. He pulled the van into the driveway.

"There doesn't seem to be anyone else here," said Peyton.

"Good. We'll have it all to ourselves." Dad got out of the van and stretched. The screen door snapped shut as they went inside.

Sunlight sprinkled through the window in little patterns on the floor. Austin smelled apple pie. No, more like turkey with mashed potatoes and gravy. No, that wasn't it. Hot dogs and potato salad and watermelon. Austin felt far away, but like he'd been here before.

Several wooden block tables covered with colored cloths were set with blue enamel plates and cups. Shelves lined the walls from floor to ceiling, and each shelf was crammed with many kinds of figures. Austin immediately saw a row of superheroes on a shelf across the room. Wow! There were five different ones of Superman.

"Hey, look at all the cool race cars on that shelf over there," said Aiden.

"There's a whole row of ceramic cats," said Peyton. A fluffy Persian cat rubbed against her legs, and she knelt down to rub his chin.

"I haven't seen so many trains since I was a boy," said father.

Mother smelled the roses in the center of the table. "These smell delicious. I wonder what kind they are. I'm surprised they grow up here, where it's so cold."

A tall, slender woman with short gray hair walked slowly around the corner from the kitchen. She wiped her hands on the long white apron that covered her clothes and smiled. "I'm Mabel. Looking for breakfast?"

"Yes, we're starving," said Mom.

"Any gas around here?" said Dad.

"Just down the road. Not far."

"What's the deluxe?" said Austin.

"Best meal you ever had." Mabel looked down at him and smiled. Austin felt warm all over, as if he had been sitting in the sun on a sandy beach.

Mabel walked back toward the kitchen. "Have a seat wherever," she called over her shoulder.

"Let's sit here. I like the pink roses best," said Peyton.

"Where's the menus?" Aiden looked around.

They sat down on wooden benches and looked around the room. Mabel brought out freshly squeezed orange juice and coffee. "This will wet your whistle." Austin sipped the orange juice, which tingled pleasantly as it went down.

Then Mabel set a plate before each of them. "Let me know if you need anything else."

"French toast with fresh berries," said Peyton. "How did she know that's my favorite?"

"This is a great-looking omelet. Look at all that ham." said Dad, "But I didn't order yet."

"Blueberry pancakes and real maple syrup." Aiden smiled at the stack of jumbo pancakes that oozed large blueberries on his plate.

"French croissants," Mom said. "And apricot jam. My favorite. But how did she know?"

Austin looked down at his macaroni and cheese and smiled. This was something his stomach could handle. It was hot and perfectly cheesy. It melted in his mouth, and contentment curled around him.

Time seemed to stand still, as they ate every bite.

"Remember that summer when we saw the seals in Maine, and Peyton drove the lobster boat?" said Aiden.

"We went around in circles." Mom laughed.

"Remember when we climbed that mountain in the Porcupine Mountains, and Aiden got to the top before all of us?" said Peyton.

"He wasn't even out of breath." Dad smiled.

"Remember when Austin jumped into cold Lake Michigan before any of the rest of us were brave enough to try it?"

"Remember when Dad couldn't find the keys to the car and Peyton found them? We were worried we would have to spend the night on the beach."

"Remember when that squirrel stole the banana from Dad's lunch?" said Austin.

"Dad couldn't figure out where it went," said Aiden. Everyone laughed.

"Remember when we were in the airport and that man dropped his wallet?"

"And when Mom caught up to him, he gave her fifty dollars." Aiden whistled.

Their plates empty, they all leaned back and smiled. Dad paid the bill, and they walked out into the clean mountain air. The sun smiled down as the fog lifted over the mountains. A gentle breeze whispered through the pine trees.

"You can sit by the window, Austin," said Aiden. "That way, maybe you won't get sick."

Austin sat by the window.

"You can lean against me if you get tired," said Peyton.

"Thanks." Austin smiled.

"Want to play favorite superhero?" said Aiden.

"Sure," said Austin. "Superman."

"Isn't this the most beautiful view?" said Mom.

Dad began to whistle "When you wish upon a star."

Austin turned around for one last look at the Dream Inn. Snow on the Green Mountains glistened in the early morning sunlight. Below the mountains, a soft mist closed in around everything, but he thought he could see the Dream Inn sign still blinking in the window.

FUN FACTS:

What are the Green Mountains?

The Green Mountains are part of the Appalachian Mountains, a range that stretches from Quebec in the north to Alabama in the south. The mountains are known for hiking and skiing.

(vermontvacation.com)

The Great Dragon Woods

"Sarina. Sarina. Get up, get up." Standing by the bed, Marissa gently shook her sister.

"What time is it?" Sarina groaned and rolled over, away from Marissa.

"We're going to Stone Castle for the great dragon hunt. Don't you remember? There will be a big feast tomorrow night with music and dancing."

Sarina opened her eyes wide and sat up. "How did I sleep so late? Are you packed already? I packed last night." She pointed to the travel case by the door.

"All packed. Paleen came in a few minutes ago. The bath is ready, and we should hurry and dress. She will bring in our breakfast in half an hour. Mother is supervising the loading of the tricart. Father is organizing the horses and what everyone will need for the hunt. The couriers will leave soon, so they will make it to the castle before we get there."

Sarina got out of bed and grabbed the clothes that had been laid out for her the night before. "I call first bath."

Marissa giggled. "Already had mine. So, second bath for you."

After her bath, Sarina put on the blue velvet traveling dress. Since she had turned fourteen years old last month and was no longer a child, she could demand help in dressing. But she didn't think she needed a lady's maid yet and didn't want to be fussed over.

Marissa set their luggage out in the hall for the porter to pick up and take down to the tricart. She stood at the window and watched the couriers rushing about in the courtyard below. The groom had brought out Swift and Ebony, her brothers' horses, and the horses stamped their feet impatiently. Marissa thought about her horse, Caramel, a small, brown mare with white feet. She had received the horse from her father last spring when she turned eleven. Marissa wished she could ride Caramel today, but her mother would insist that she ride in the carriage, so she wouldn't mess up her hair or her clothes.

Into a tapestry bag Sarina packed a few things for the long drive to their country castle — a book that she was eager to read, a drawing box with paper and a piece of charcoal, and a pack of cards to entertain Marissa when she got restless, as she always did when they rode in the carriage. She smiled, glad to be traveling. Summer vacation at the annual dragon hunt was always exciting. People came from all over the kingdom. She thought about who she might dance with. Maybe she would meet someone new and interesting.

Marissa turned from the window and gestured to Sarina's packed bag. "Oh, good, you're ready. I can't wait to get started."

As they hurried down the long, winding stairway, they glimpsed the bright sunlight that streamed through the windows of the castle. At the bottom of the stairs, Paleen stood in the large entryway, directing the porters as to what was fragile and where to put things on the tricart. Their mother stood beside her, making sure everything they would need had been packed. She looked them over and nodded her approval at the neatness of their appearance.

"May we go outside and watch the packing?" Marissa tilted her head and looked at her mother.

Their mother smiled. "Yes, of course, but don't get in the way and don't get your clothes mussed up. You will want to look respectable when we arrive at Stone Castle."

Sarina and Marissa stepped outside onto the marble porch that spanned the front of the castle. Large, white pillars along the edge of the porch held up the roof above it. Vines of purple flowers cascaded down along the ends of the porch, sending out a scent of cinnamon.

Their oldest brother Devlen nodded to them but continued to watch the packing activity. Finden, who was between Sarina and Marissa in age, called to them.

"We're going dragon hunting! I'm going to find one this year for sure."

Sarina laughed. "Should be fun."

"Will they really hunt a dragon? I have never seen them bring one back, but they have big stories to tell." Marissa looked at her sister.

Sarina shook her head. "It's just an excuse to have a big party and to honor our ancestors who did hunt dragons. I don't think anyone has actually seen a dragon in many years."

"I would like to see a dragon. Do you think they would be ferocious? Would they let you pet them if you were friendly?"

"The stories people tell always describe them as ferocious, but I don't know if anyone today really knows what dragons were like in the old days."

When everything was packed, two of the grooms climbed onto the tricart and set off for the castle, hoping to reach it soon enough to unload before the family arrived. The carriage driver helped Sarina, Marissa, and their mother climb into the carriage and clucked to the horses. Four matching white horses pulled the carriage at a brisk pace. Their father, the King, and his two squires, rode ahead of the carriage. Finden and Devlen followed on their horses.

Marissa gazed out the window of the carriage. Sarina pulled out the book she had brought and began to read. Their mother leaned back in the seat and closed her eyes. As the sun rose to the top of the sky, the group halted to water the horses and eat lunch. The servants had arrived ahead of the family. They spread cloths on the ground and served platters of bread, cheese, meats, fruits, and cakes.

After lunch, the entourage continued on toward the castle. Suddenly, they heard a crack, and the front left corner of their carriage lurched to the ground.

"Ouch!" Sarina bumped her arm on the side of the carriage.

"Everyone okay?" Devlen and Finden reined in their horses beside the carriage and dismounted.

Her mother examined Sarina's arm carefully. "Sarina's arm is sore, but we are okay."

Father and his squires turned and rode back to the carriage. Marissa was already climbing out. Devlen carefully helped Sarina and his mother to climb down.

The carriage driver looked at the damage and shook his head. "The axle is broken at the wheel. Can't be fixed. The carriage was checked over carefully before we left. I don't know what could have happened. We will have to send someone to the castle to bring back another carriage."

The King called to his two squires and directed them to ride ahead and return with another carriage. He assured them that the family would be perfectly safe. There was little crime in the kingdom, and he had his two sons with him. The squires nodded and urged their horses to a fast trot down the road.

"Let's not wait here. There is a manor house not far away where we can wait, and I think a walk would benefit all of us."

The King nodded to his wife. "As you wish. I will walk my horse, and you and I can walk together. Devlen and Finden, you walk along with Sarina and Marissa."

The six of them started off down the road at a leisurely pace. Their parents led the way, and Devlen and Finden strode quickly along behind them. Marissa and Sarina followed more slowly, admiring the flowers that carpeted the woods on either side.

Dark clouds suddenly covered the sun, and large raindrops plopped upon their heads. Thunder rumbled in the distance, and rain poured down.

"Take cover in the woods." The King gestured toward the trees. He took the Queen's hand, and they hurried into the woods on the left side of the path. The brothers followed them. Marissa and Sarina dashed into the woods on the right side of the path.

Sarina stopped running and looked in all directions. Marissa was still beside her, but she could not see the road. She thought she could hear her brothers calling, as if they were trying to find them. But the voices were very faint, and she wasn't sure that she heard them at all.

Enormous trees towered over them. Their crooked branches crowded the space, casting dark shadows onto the path. The wind in the trees whispered, as if people were talking to one another.

"I think we're lost. These trees don't look familiar." Marissa moved closer to Sarina.

"But how can we be lost? Where did everyone go?" Sarina shivered. How had this happened? The carriage had broken a axle, the king and queen had decided that the family should walk to the nearby manor house and stay with friends until another carriage could come for them. Their father and mother and their brothers were walking just ahead of them.

Then the rain poured down, and everyone ran. One minute their family was there, and then they weren't.

"Which way should we go?" Marissa's voice quavered, and she grasped her sister's hand.

"Let's find a place to sit here for a few minutes. When they don't see us, someone will surely come to find us." Sarina looked around for a place they could wait. She spied a bench made of willow branches placed underneath a tree with large, heart-shaped leaves.

"Come on, we can sit there for a few minutes." She pointed toward the bench and tugged on Marissa's hand. Marissa followed her to the bench and sat down. Above them the leaves gently swayed, and a soft wind fanned their faces. It was not raining here, but the leaves grew so thickly that they could not see the sky.

In the branches above their heads, the leaves rustled. Sarina looked up. A brown, furry animal about four feet long crept slowly along a large branch. It looked down at them with big, brown eyes and spoke in a slow, deep voice. "Who. Are. You?"

Sarina shook her head. Was she hearing things? Was that animal really talking to her?

At the sound of the voice, Marissa looked up. "Wow! How great! A talking sloth! I've never seen one before. I remember seeing one in that book about ancient animals. Remember?" Marissa smiled. "Hello, my name is Marissa, and this is my sister Sarina. "What's your name?"

"Speed. O. Thanks. For. Ask. Ing."

Marissa stopped herself from laughing. She did not want to insult the sloth and drive him away. Although at the rate he was moving, it would take him a while to move anywhere.

"Do you know where we are? Where does this path lead?" If the animal was talking, maybe it could help them.

"You. Are. In. The. Great. Dragon. Woods. This. Path. Leads. To. The. Home. Of. The. Master. Wizard."

Before Sarina could ask anything else, the sloth closed its eyes and began to snore.

"This won't do. We should just keep walking down the road. We will certainly catch up to everyone. Or, at least we will find someone who can tell us how to get to Stone Castle." She took Marissa's hand and pulled her to her feet.

"Who is the Master Wizard? I have never heard of him."

"There is no such person. Just a story from a talking sloth." Sarina laughed. "This is all ridiculous."

Marissa wasn't so sure. The sloth seemed real enough. She followed Sarina along the road in the direction they had been going. The giant trees crowded the path and branches crossed over their heads. They did not meet anyone or encounter any more animals.

"This is kind of creepy." Marissa frowned.

Sarina stopped. "This doesn't look right." Along both sides of the path, tall, rounded bushes had replaced the trees. Their black blossoms the size of cantaloupes emitted a strong scent of garlic. The odor was strong, stifling. Sarina wrinkled her nose.

"What's that sound?" Marissa touched Sarina's arm.

Sarina listened. A raspy buzzing sound grew louder. Suddenly, a swarm of wasps as large as grapefruits headed towards them. They were bright yellow with black stripes and large, bulging eyes. Their buzzing grew louder as they came nearer.

"Help!" Marissa looked around for a place to hide.

"There! Come on!" Sarina screamed and began running. Marissa raced after her. Sarina reached a narrow building that looked like a tool shed, yanked open the door, pulled Marissa in behind her, and slammed it. The only light inside filtered through a small, dusty window at the top of the door. Marissa and Sarina covered their ears to mask the overwhelming sound. Thwack! Thwack!

"They're trying to get in! What should we do?" Marissa shuddered.

Through the small window at the top of the door, they could see a large eye looking in at them. The buzzing and thwacking continued. Frantically, Sarina looked around for something to put in front of the door to keep them out. She grabbed a small three-legged stool and wedged it against the door.

Marissa began to cry. "I think one of them stung me." She looked down at her leg. A large, red welt had swelled up on the back of her leg.

"Oh, no! Does it hurt a lot?"

Marissa cried harder. Sarina felt like crying, too.

"Listen." No more buzzing and thwacking. "I think they left." Sarina peered through the small window. She didn't see any sign of the wasps, so she opened the door a crack and peered out.

"Are they gone?" Marissa sniffed.

"I think so. Can you walk? I think we should get out of these bushes with the weird flowers." Sarina looked around the tool shed and picked up a small shovel. She handed a trowel to Marissa. "In case they come back. We will be able to fight them off." She wasn't sure if that was true, but didn't want to stay here any longer.

They stepped out of the shed and looked around. They saw no sign of the wasps. Helping Marissa as much as she could, Sarina hurried them along the road past the bushes of the black flowers.

And suddenly the forest changed again. The bushes disappeared, and the air no longer smelled of garlic. Drooping branchlets of giant weeping willow trees swayed gently along the ground.

Sarina felt exhausted, frustrated, helpless. She looked at Marissa and could see that she could not go any farther.

"Let's get underneath one of these trees. No one will be able to see us, and we can rest for a while."

Marissa nodded, holding back her tears.

Sarina pushed some branchlets aside to let Marissa get under them. She could see that Marissa's leg had swollen more. Marissa collapsed onto the soft, mossy ground underneath the tree. Sarina sat beside her and put her arm around her.

"Someone is singing a lullaby." Marissa closed her eyes.

Sarina listened. She could hear it, too. But she could not understand the words. She suddenly felt drowsy and closed her eyes. Soon they were both asleep.

When Sarina opened her eyes, she gasped. She stared into the dark blue eyes of a unicorn who was nuzzling her with its nose.

"Don't be alarmed." The unicorn stepped back a couple of paces. "Just checking to make sure you are alive. It seems that you are."

Marissa opened her eyes. "Oh, how grand! I've always wanted to see a unicorn!"

"But there aren't any unicorns in our woods."

"Perhaps these are not your woods." The unicorn tilted its head to one side and watched them.

"Do you know where we are? How can we get out of these woods?"

"Perhaps you should talk to the Master Wizard. He may be able to help you. Just follow the path that way." The unicorn pointed the horn on her head in the direction they should go, and disappeared into the woods.

"We have to get out of here. It will be dark soon." Sarina tried to keep her voice steady.

"Hey, look, my leg isn't swollen anymore. And it doesn't hurt." Marissa smiled and got to her feet. She rubbed the spot where she had been stung. There wasn't even a mark.

"That's amazing. How could that happen?"

"Maybe the unicorn used some magic on it before we woke up."

"I am glad your leg is fine. But I don't understand any of this." Sarina shook her head. "Come on." She stood up and parted the branchlets they had hidden behind. They were surrounded by other large trees with branchlets like the tree they had chosen to hide them. All the branchlets seemed to sway gently, although Sarina did not notice that there was any breeze. The sun shone brightly in an azure sky, but she could see that it was late afternoon. Perhaps the sloth and the unicorn were right. This wasn't their woods. But who did it belong to? And how did she and Marissa get here?

The path ahead of them seemed wider. They walked out of the forest of willow trees into a more open area with tall, straight birch trees. The white bark of the trees gleamed in the sun, and birds called from the canopy of leaves.

"Haven't we walked far enough? Why hasn't anyone found us?" Marissa grumbled.

"That's a good question. I am not sure we are going in the right direction, but I think we should keep walking. We will come to a house or farm or village sometime."

The forest changed again to close-standing evergreens, cedars, and many kinds of firs. Marisa grabbed Sarina's arm. "Did you hear that?"

Sarina listened. There it was. A heavy thud, thud, thud, as if large feet stomped through the trees. Where was it coming from? What was it? In the trees on the left of the path, branches began to sway back and forth, and the thuds continued. Something that sounded large. Very large. She grabbed Marissa's hand and pulled her behind a large oak tree that looked out of place in this part of the woods. They peered around the huge tree trunk, as whatever it was stayed hidden and continued walking through the trees until the thuds became fainter.

They hurried down the path, almost running, sometimes looking behind them to be sure they weren't being followed by something or someone.

Sellen put down his wand and frowned. He shook his head and tried to think. What had he forgotten? What had gone wrong?

"Did it work? Were you able to weave the protective spell as you hoped?" Michard looked at Sellen.

"I don't think so. I felt the spell taking hold, and then it faded. I will have to try again. I will check the spells and try again tonight. I have to do it successfully by midnight."

"True. True. I don't envy you, being the apprentice and all."

"I felt honored to be chosen by the Master Wizard out of all of us who were the right age to be trained."

"When he tested us, you showed the most magical ability."

"I hope I will be worthy of it. He taught me a lot of what he knew, but he died before he taught me everything."

"Don't worry. You'll figure it out. And there are some on the Council who know some magic and can advise you." Michard patted Sellen on the shoulder.

They walked in silence for a few minutes until Michard halted suddenly. He pointed to the two sisters who were coming towards them on the path. Sellen stopped and looked where his friend pointed. "Who are they?"

Sarina looked up. She paused and put a hand on Marissa's arm. She didn't know these two young men on the path ahead of them. Still, they had to ask directions from someone. "Stay beside me. We will have to talk to them."

"Hello, are you lost?" Sellen and Michard stood and waited for the sisters to come closer.

"Hello. We are looking for Stone Castle. Do you know where it is? Are we going in the right direction?" Sarina stood up straight and tried to speak with confidence. That was the best way to deal with strangers, she thought.

The boys looked puzzled. "How did you get here? This is not the way to the Stone Castle."

"My sister and I are on our way to the Great Dragon Hunt. We don't want to miss all the fun." Sarina smiled.

Michard looked at Sellen and raised his eyebrows. Sellen shook his head slightly with a warning look in his eyes.

"Can you help us find our way, or not?" Sarina wasn't sure they could trust these boys. Why were they acting so strangely?

"I think you will have to come with us back to our home. It will be dark soon, and we will not be able to get you to your castle before nighttime. Perhaps we can get you there safely tomorrow." Sellen tried to smile to reassure them. He did not mean them any harm. He would like them to go on their way, but that would not be possible until the Council had made a decision about the strangers. The strangers clearly did not know about the dragons.

Sarina did not move from where she stood. What did he mean about taking them home? They just wanted to get to the castle. Their parents would be worried.

Sellen whistled a phrase of pure, clear notes. Suddenly, a bird appeared and settled on Sellen's shoulder. It was blue with a tufted orange crest on its head and wings tipped in lemon yellow.

"Ooh, is that your pet bird? Does it have a name?" Marissa stared.

"She is not a pet. Her name is known only to the other birds." Sellen smiled at her. "We sometimes help each other out." He whistled another tune and the bird flew away.

Sarina said nothing. This forest was full of strange and amazing things. Perhaps she was only dreaming and would wake up in the castle. But it all felt far too real.

"Don't worry. My mother will make sure you have everything you need, and tomorrow we will show you the way out of these woods." Sellen hoped the sisters would be able to leave, but they would have to keep a secret.

"We will go with you and meet your mother." Sarina hoped she could convince his mother to show them the way out of these weird woods.

"Come." Michard smiled at them. It wasn't so bad to have a pretty girl to talk to. "You will love Sellen's estate. It is the prettiest one in the woods."

As the four of them walked along together, Sarina tried to find out more about Sellen and Michard. Sellen walked along quietly. He seemed deep in thought. Michard was eager to talk.

"We are both studying at the University, and sometimes we go out to practice what we have learned, so we can perfect what we know."

"And what have you learned?" Sarina was curious. Her oldest brother had recently finished his studies and now spent time with their father learning how to manage their family's properties.

"Oh, this and that. How to do things, you know. What about you? What are you studying?"

"My mother believes that women should learn a variety of subjects. Marissa and I are both studying literature, geography, history, languages, art, and music. At different levels, of course."

"And science, of course," Marissa added. "My favorite."

"Your mother is wise." Sellen looked at her and smiled. His sisters studied the same subjects that he and Michard had studied at their ages.

They soon reached Sellen's estate. A grand three-story house made of sandy colored stone glowed in the evening sun. Large windows across the front of it looked out on gardens that were filled with many-colored flowers. In the center of the gardens was a bright blue pool with a stream that flowed into it from the woods behind the house. Beyond the gardens, the trees in a large orchard drooped with many fruits of different kinds.

"Oh, this is beautiful." Marissa looked around with delight.

A tall, elegant woman came out of the house and down the steps. She was dressed in a simple silk dress of deep lilac. Behind her, two girls skipped down the steps. They were both younger than Sellen, but tall like their mother. One was dark-haired like her, and the other fair-haired like Sellen.

"Here comes my mother and my two sisters. My brothers are not here just now, but you will meet them at the feast. "I will introduce you to my sisters, and they will be sure you are comfortable. There is a feast and festival tonight, so you will be well entertained while you are here."

Sellen's mother greeted them warmly. His sisters immediately began asking them questions about where they were from, what they liked to do, what were their favorite dances.

"Hey, give them a chance to settle in." Sellen laughed.

Sellen's mother led Sarina and Marissa into the house. The entryway was vast, and many colorful paintings hung on the walls. Sarina hoped she would have a chance to look at the paintings later.

The sisters were shown upstairs into a large room with a canopied bed with a coverlet of rose and mint green. Windows filled one wall, with a door in the middle that opened onto a balcony. Through the windows Sarina could see the gardens near the house and the woods in the distance.

"Come down whenever you wish. If you are tired and desire a nap, someone will come to wake you before the feast begins".

Marissa lay down on the soft bed and soon fell asleep. Sarina laid beside her, but got up after a few minutes and went out onto the balcony. She was uneasy. Could they trust Sellen to show them where they needed to go tomorrow? Or would he try to keep them here for some reason she did not understand?

When Marissa woke, the sisters washed up and combed their hair as best they could. After a couple of wrong turns, they found their way downstairs. Following the sound of voices, they found everyone in the back garden. Several long tables had been set up along the rose garden. Servers carried out platters piled high with food.

Guests started to arrive, talking and laughing as they greeted people they knew. Sarina and Marissa stood off to one side, unsure of what they should do. They didn't know anyone and weren't sure they belonged here.

"Hey, there you are." Michard joined them with a big smile on his face. "Come on, I want to introduce you to my brothers and some friends." He started off toward a small group of people, turning to be sure they followed him.

Michard's two brothers were a bit younger than him, but just as friendly and talkative. Sarina and Marissa relaxed and joined in the conversation.

"Time to sit down for feasting and speeches." Sellen strode up and stood beside them. He guided them to a table where his family was sitting. Michard's family sat with them as well.

Heaping platters of colorful ripe fruits and vegetables that the sisters had never tried, many kinds of meats, bowls of stews and casseroles of many flavors. Marissa's favorites were the plates of cakes, pies, and pastries.

A group of musicians began to play, and people drifted off to the dance floor that had been laid down at the end of the garden. Sarina did not expect to dance, as she had not been properly introduced to anyone. Unlike the gatherings at Stone Castle, everyone danced, and it all seemed much less formal than feasts at home. Michard invited her to dance and made her laugh as he tried to teach her the favorite dances. He introduced her to a friend, and after that she hardly sat down. She was pleased to see Marissa swept into a group of boys and girls her age who danced together in a group dance of their own making. She looked around for Sellen, but did not see him. Did he not dance?

The evening sun cast shadows when Sarina finally sat down on a bench in the garden to catch her breath and think about what she and her sister should do. Marissa saw her and came over and stood beside her.

"This is more fun than the dance at the dragon hunt feast. Everyone is relaxed and friendly."

"Yes, it is." Sarina spied Sellen standing off by himself under a tree. "Oh, there he is. I need to speak with him. She stood and walked over to him. Marissa followed her.

"Thank you for your hospitality. May I ask you a question?"

Sellen turned to her and smiled. "I hope you are having a good time. Yes, of course, ask me your question."

"Do you intend to lead us where we need to go tomorrow?"

"Yes, I do. It would be wrong to keep you here. I have spoken with the Council, and they are agreed that I should show you the way home tomorrow."

"Would the Council decide not to let us go home?" Sarina frowned.

"Come with me. Let me show you something."

"Okay." Sarina looked at Marissa and nodded. There was a secret of some kind and she wanted to know what it was.

"I will ask Michard to come with us." Sarina and Marissa waited while Sellen found Michard and spoke to him quietly. Michard looked surprised, but nodded his agreement. Before they started off, Sellen and Michard each picked up a bag from the orchard and slung it over his shoulder.

Sellen set off toward the woods behind the house, and the others followed. Michard smiled encouragement to the sisters, but no one spoke as they walked on a pine-needle path through the woods. The moon shone down through the trees, sprinkling flashes of gold as the leaves swayed gently in the warm breeze. Wildflowers scented the air. The woods were quiet, except for rustlings among the trees and the occasional call of owls.

Sarina felt they had been walking a long time and worried about where Sellen might lead them. He had said he would help them to get home tomorrow. Could she trust him?

Suddenly, Sellen stopped and put his finger to his lips. He stepped out from the trees, and the three others stepped out quietly beside him. They stood in a large green, grassy field.

"Oh!" Both sisters whispered at the same time.

Five giant animals grazed, while two smaller ones chased each other around the field. The larger ones were covered with brown, scaly skins. Their wings were folded, and they gently swished their long tails in the grass. The two smaller ones were a dark green.

"Are those dragons?" Sarina could hardly believe what she was seeing. "Where did they come from? Why are they here?"

"Are they ferocious? Would they eat us?" Marissa's eyes looked very large in the moonlight, and she stood very close to her older sister.

Michard laughed. "No, they are never ferocious, unless they are protecting themselves and their families. "

"I will tell you about the dragons," Sellen began. "These woods belong to the Master Wizard. Many years ago, nearly all the dragons were killed off during the hunting seasons. The Master Wizard found two of them, hiding in a cave. He decided to put a magic protection spell around the dragons to keep them safe, and he encouraged them to live in his woods. The dragons wander throughout the forest whenever they wish, but they spend most of their time here. Now, there are many dragons in our woods. At this time year the Wizard always performed the spell of protection." Sellen looked at them.

"So, the Wizard saved the dragons."

"That's it." Sellen smiled. "But the Master Wizard died suddenly. I was his only apprentice, so I have taken his place. Since he is no longer here, I cast the spell of protection for the first time this afternoon. Unfortunately, my spell did not go quite right. I believe that I ended up catching the two of you in it instead. Tonight, I must go out and try the spell again. It must be successful tonight, so that the dragons will not wander out of these woods and be killed in the annual dragon hunt. If I do not protect them, they will soon be hunted to extinction, like what happened in the past. They are beautiful and a sight to see."

Sellen looked at Sarina and Marissa. "I have looked through all of the spell books of the Master Wizard, and think I know what went wrong the first time. But if you tell anyone what you have learned, the dragons may no longer be safe. The Council and I have decided that I must help you return to your home and trust that you will keep our secret."

"We would never tell, would we, Sarina?" Marissa shook her head. "The dragons are too wonderful to be killed."

"We will keep your secret. The great dragon hunt has not caught any dragons for years, so I don't think anyone will actually miss it." Sarina smiled at Sellen. "Would the dragons let us get closer, or would that not be safe?"

"They are wary of strangers, and we have tried to keep them that way, so they will be safe from being trapped and captured. But they know Michard and me well. We will call to the small ones who are only one year old. They are very playful, so we will be careful."

Sellen and Michard both whistled. All of the dragons looked up, but only the two small ones came racing over. Up close, they did not look small! They still towered over Sarina and Marissa. With large, expressive green eyes they stared at the sisters.

"I call this one Prancer, and Michard named that one Dancer. Sellen opened the bag and poured out a variety of fruits on the ground. The two dragons immediately pounced on the fruit. Prancer chose a large watermelon and bit a chunk out of it. Juice ran down his chin and he stuck out his long tongue and licked it off. Dancer chose three oranges at once and loudly chomped them down.

"When they finish eating, they will feel playful and will let you touch them if you wish."

They watched the dragons eagerly eat the rest of the fruit. Prancer nudged Marissa, and she gently touched the dragon's side. "Ooh, its skin is not scaly, like I iexpected." The dragon hummed as if she enjoyed the touch, and Marissa petted her gently.

"They do not get their scales until they are older."

The other dragon nudged Sarina. She laughed. "Okay, I guess you want to be petted, too." She ran her hand gently along his side.

"Is that all they eat, just fruit?" Marissa looked at Sellen.

"Oh, no. They are free to roam through the woods to eat whatever they want, but they know that someone will be here in the evening to provide them with the fruit that they love so much."

"When we were walking through the woods, we heard loud, thudding footsteps through the trees, but we didn't see anything. Could that have been a dragon?" Marissa looked at her sister.

"Probably. They are shy of strangers, so they may have been checking you out and didn't want to be seen."

"That was probably a good thing," Sarina laughed. "We would have been terrified, I think."

When the dragons had eaten all the fruit, they nudged Sellen and Michard.

"Okay, okay!" Michard grabbed a yellow ball from under a tree and tossed it into the field.

Prancer and Dancer raced after it and kicked it back and forth, as they ran around the field. After a few minutes they stopped and flopped down in the grass.

"Wow! Thanks! That was so great!" Marissa grinned.

"I will never forget meeting the dragons. If I ever wake up, that is." Sarina laughed.

"You aren't dreaming." Sellen smiled at her. "I will make sure you find your way to your castle first thing tomorrow morning. But now Michard will take you back to the party, while I perform the spell that will keep the dragons safe."

Marissa and Sarina followed Michard back to the feast and dancing. Guests were starting to say goodbye and leave the garden.

"You must be tired from your adventures today." Sellen's mother came up beside them. Sarina and Marissa nodded. Sellen's sisters showed them how to get back to their room, and they both slept soundly until the early morning sun sprinkled shadows on the floor.

After they were dressed and had eaten a quick breakfast, they said goodbye to Sellen's family and all the people they had met.

"Thank you for your generous hospitality. We had a lovely time." Sarina shook hands with everyone.

"Come. We will ride to the edge of the forest that borders Stone Castle." Sellen smiled, and he and Michard helped the sisters to mount horses.

It was a short ride to the edge of the forest. Here the trees were dense, and they could not see beyond them. They all dismounted. Sellen kissed Sarina and Marissa on both cheeks, placed his hands on their shoulders and recited:

"We love to visit

But now we know

Home is where

We want to go.

I think when you walk to the other side of these trees, you will find your family on the road, not far from where you left them."

"Will we ever find our way to these woods again?" Sarina felt tears in her eyes.

"I would love to see the dragons again." Marissa looked at Sellen and Michard.

"I will come and find you, if you come to this spot at any time in the future and say the following:

A good friendship never ends.

Dragons make the best of friends."

"We will see you again then." Sarina hugged them both, and Marissa hugged them, too.

The trees lifted their branches, creating a space between them. Holding hands, the sisters walked between the trees. When they turned to look back, the trees had closed up, and they could no longer see into Dragon Woods. They stepped onto the road they had left when it started to rain and looked around. A few yards ahead of them, their parents and their two brothers stood in the road, calling their names.

"We're here!" Marissa called. She and Sarina hurried to catch up to their family.

"I worried that maybe you had gotten lost in the woods." Their mother smiled and hugged them.

Marissa and Sarina looked at each other and tried not to laugh.

FUN FACTS:

Were there ever any dragons?

There is no evidence that dragons ever existed, but they appear in legends around the world. The first dragon myths appear in the Sumerian legends. In about 2700 B.C. Dragons appear in Chinese and Indian legends. Asian dragons are often benign — bringing rain, revealing treasures or granting wishes. Chinese dragons are very powerful, and are often accompanied by lightning and thunder when they fly. The Aztecs had a legendary dragon that looked like a snake. In England, the classic dragon story of St. George rescuing a princess dates from A.D. 315. Alaskan Inuits have legends of the kikituk, a seagoing reptile that walks ashore hunting humans.

(<u>Dragons, A Brief History Long in Miles</u>, Donald G. McNeil, Jr., New York Times Science, April 29, 2003)

What is a sloth?

Tree sloths live in the tropical rainforests of South America and Central America. They spend most of their lives hanging upside down in the trees. Their slowness allows them to exist on a low-energy diet of leaves, fruit, and sap and protects them from hawks and cats that hunt by sight. Surprisingly, sloths are strong swimmers. During the Pleistocene Era, there were sloths as large as elephants, but today sloths are only 24 to 31 inches long.

(<u>Top Ten Facts About Sloths</u>, WWF-UK)

Up in a Balloon

"Mom, where are we going on vacation this year? You haven't said." My birthday is at the end of July and my mom and dad and me usually go somewhere on vacation. One time we rented a house on Lake Superior, another time we drove to Minnesota and camped out on a lake for a week. We went swimming every day, and Dad and I rented a boat and went fishing.

"We're doing something different this year, but just as fun. We're going to have a staycation." Mom looked up from the bread she was cutting for toast and smiled. She put slices of bread in the toaster.

I took another sip of orange juice. "What's a staycation?" I wasn't sure I liked the sound of it. Wasn't that the same as staying home?

"We're going to stay home and do fun things around here."

"How come?"

"We need to spend money on some repairs to the house, and your dad wants to have some time to do them."

My dad is a really good builder, and he can build anything. But most of the time he is building things for other people. He's the best builder in the world, so I knew he would want to work on our house himself.

"So, what would we do around here?"

"We'll do special things together close to home, like visit the museum at the college, go to the beach, AND take a ride in a hot air balloon."

"Are you serious?" I didn't think Mom would trick me, but still. I've wanted to go up in a hot air balloon since I saw *Around the World in 80 Days*. I've wanted to travel far, far away, like they did in the TV show. But Mom told me people don't usually go that far in a hot air balloon. I wanted to try it, though.

"Just like your uncle promised you when you were eight, he bought tickets for your tenth birthday to ride in a hot air balloon."

"Wow, that's super! I thought he was just joking, or had forgotten he said that." I jumped up from the table and hugged my mom. My uncle doesn't have any of his own kids yet, so he likes to do things for me.

It was still three days to my birthday. I was going to be in double digits this year. I didn't know how I could wait that long to be ten or to fly in a hot air balloon!

But we had still had two days before we could go up in a balloon. What would we do? Mom had made plans. She said our staycation would start tomorrow.

The first day was sunny with blue skies and nice and warm. I invited my best friend Riley to go with us to the beach. Mom packed a lunch of my favorite picnic foods, bread and cheese cubes, strawberries, grape leaves, and cookies. We had to drive awhile to get there, but Mom gave my friend and me a set of tiny board games we could play in the car. So, we didn't get bored at all. And when we got to the beach, she gave us each a set of really cool beach toys with fun shapes to build castles and stuff.

The sand was hot, so my friend and I ran across the dune and down to the water as soon as Dad parked the car. Lake Michigan stretched out for miles and miles. We dropped our towels and stuff on the beach and stuck our toes in the water. It felt cold.

Small waves rolled into shore, which is how I like it when I come to the beach. My friend and I ran right in and dove under the water. We jumped up out of the water when the cold hit us, but just laughed, and started to ride the waves.

Mom and Dad came in the water for a while with a beach ball, and we all played catch. Then Dad grabbed the ball, and we played keep-away, with the three of us chasing him and getting the ball back. And then he pretended to be a shark, and we screamed in fun.

Mom suggested we rest for a while and unpacked the lunch.

After we ate, my friend and I built an enormous sand castle with eight turrets. Dad helped us to dig a moat around it. Then we flopped onto our towels and felt the warmth of the sun toast us.

On the second day of our staycation, Mom and I went to the museum at the college. There is always an exhibit of Indigenous art and lots of other cool things. One of my favorites is a stuffed polar bear (although I am sorry that he is stuffed) and a family of plaster penguins, with a baby one between its mom's feet. I like to look at the birchbark canoe and imagine what it would be like to paddle it down the river a long time ago, when there were lots of trees and animals and not many people. I also always look at the glass case with a display of Indigenous beadwork. Indigenous people create beautiful jewelry with very tiny, colorful beads. Sometimes they make designs, and sometimes they make things like flowers.

When we got worn out from looking at so much stuff, Mom took me out for lunch at my favorite restaurant. Pizza, of course. The crust was thin and crispy, there were lots of vegetables on it, and the cheese was nice and gooey. I also got to have dessert, a hot fudge sundae. Staycations aren't so bad after all.

The day of my birthday, I woke up early. Finally, the day was here. I just couldn't sleep because I was so excited. I went into my parents' room to see if they were awake, but Mom said to go back to sleep. It was balloon day! How could anyone sleep? I tried to go back to sleep, but of course I couldn't. I played a game on my laptop and hoped everyone would get up soon.

I heard Mom in the kitchen fixing breakfast. I jumped out of bed and ran into the kitchen. Something smelled really good.

"Happy Birthday! You ready for a balloon ride?" Mom smiled and gave me a big hug. She was excited, too.

Just then, dad came into the kitchen. "Happy Birthday, kiddo."

I hugged my dad. "Are you excited about the balloon ride?"

"I don't think I would like being up in an open basket like that, but I am excited to watch you do it. I'll be there just in case you came down in a tree or something." He smiled.

I laughed. He was just joking me up. He didn't really think we would come down in a tree. Did he?

Mom fixed my favorite breakfast, pumpkin pancakes. With whipped cream. "Yum," I said.

Dad handed me two books wrapped in colorful paper with balloons on it. "To open when we have cake and ice cream later. Just so you have something to open on your birthday."

We had to wait until afternoon to take the balloon ride, so Mom packed a lunch for my friend Addi from next door and me. I went over and knocked on her door. She opened it right away.

"Happy birthday." She handed me a small present. "Open it."

Sometimes I feel shy about opening presents, but I took off the paper and looked inside. "Thanks. I really wanted this set of gel pens. We can try them out later."

"You're welcome."

"You want to ride to the park? Mom packed a lunch."

"Sure. Just a sec." She asked her mom if she could go and came outside.

We rode our bikes to the park, which is only a few blocks from our houses. There is a great playground with swings and climbing stuff and a wooden boat you can pretend to drive. We swung high on the swings and pretended we were in a hot air balloon, floating far away. We described all the places we might see, like the Grand Canyon and alligators in the Florida Everglades. Then we climbed up the rope ladder and pretended we were pirates on the boat. We found buried treasure on a deserted island. We sat under a tree and ate the lunch Mom packed. Then we rode home.

"Can't wait to hear all about your balloon ride. Are you scared?"

"No, not really. It'll be great! I'll come over and tell you all about it." I waved and raced home.

Mom and Dad and I got ready to go to the balloon launch. I wasn't sure what to wear. It was a warm day, but would it be cold up there or hot? Mom said, just take a jacket.

We got to the field where the balloon would go up a bit early, so we could watch how they put it all together. The balloon was lying flat out on the ground,

"How will they get it up?" I looked at Mom. I hadn't thought the balloon would be so flat.

"Propane burners make the air hot. They will pump it up soon, I think."

The basket lay on its side, attached to the balloon by ropes. It looked tiny next to the balloon. I was a little nervous, but could hardly wait to get into it.

Pretty soon the balloon started to blow up, as they pumped hot air into it. When the balloon got enough hot air, it puffed up really big and pulled the basket upright. The balloon was colorful with red, green, blue and yellow squares. Right away I noticed there were words on it, "Captain Phogg Balloon Rides."

Phineas Phogg, just like *Around the World in 80 Days*. I knew this captain wasn't the real Phineas Phogg. Still, that was cool.

The balloon was still held to the ground by ropes and we were asked to climb aboard. The balloon crew helped Mom and I get in, along with several other people. There wasn't a ladder or anything. Dad took our picture as we smiled and waved.

The crew started untying the ropes and the basket wobbled slightly. The basket and balloon began to rise. I saw my dad waving, way down there on the ground. We were floating in the sky, just like I imagined it would be! I looked up into the giant balloon that rose above us, into a rainbow of colors. Fire flamed up in the center, blowing to keep the balloon up there. It felt very hot on my back. I hadn't expected that. So, I took off my jacket.

The sky was so blue and the sun shone so brightly. Fluffy clouds drifted above us. They looked close enough that I could reach out and touch them. A bird flew by so close to us that I could see each of its feathers. A hawk, Mom said.

We floated along and I took some pictures. Far below, I spied green trees and different colored houses and lots of lakes of different sizes. Some of them looked blue and some more gray. Tiny cars zoomed along the roads. I could see for miles and miles.

I closed my eyes just for a few minutes and imagined we floated across mountains and cities like Paris and London on our way to some exciting place no one had ever been before. I spotted another balloon, blue with red stripes.

In way too short a time I felt the balloon start to drift downward. I wanted to say, "Wait, let's keep going. So much to see." But I didn't. I could see Dad below us, running towards the balloon. He had followed the balloon in the car. As we came down, Dad helped the crew to pull the balloon down and push out the air.

One of the men helped us all to climb out. I felt a little shaky standing on solid ground. We stayed and watched as they folded the balloon up and stuffed it all into a big bag.

"How long were we up in the air?"

"Almost an hour, I think." Dad smiled at me.

That was amazing. It felt like we were up there just a few minutes. On the way home I couldn't stop talking about how cool it was to float through the air, and couldn't we get our own hot air balloon, so we could go up whenever we wanted?

When we got home, Dad and I played a game while Mom frosted my birthday cake. Before she was finished, the doorbell rang. I ran to get it and it was my grandparents! I was so surprised because I did not know they were coming. I gave them both a big hug.

"Hey, guess who's here!" I called to my parents.

"Maybe your grandparents?" Mom and Dad said together and laughed. I guess they were in on the secret all along. Anyway, my grandparents had to drive awhile to get here, so they will stay the night and will be here tomorrow.

After dinner we had cake and ice cream. And, my birthday cake was in the shape of a balloon! I made a wish and blew out the candles. But it's a secret because I want it to come true. My grandparents gave me a soccer ball, because I am going to play on a soccer team for the first time in the fall, and now I can practice up. Could a birthday get any better?

One of the books Dad gave me is *Around the World in 80 Days*. It was written a lot of years ago by this guy named Jules

Verne. When I read it, I will remember how it feels to be up there floating along in the sky. If you ever get the chance to do it, I definitely recommend a hot air balloon ride. Even though you won't get to go around the world.

FUN FACTS:

Do people really go up in balloons?

Yes, there are companies that offer hot-air balloon rides and take people up from certain places. There are also balloon festivals where lots of balloons go up at once.

Who was Jules Verne?

Jules Gabriel Verne was a French novelist, poet, and playwright. He is best known for writing *Twenty Thousand Leagues Under the Sea*, *Around the World in Eighty Days*, and *Journey to the Center of the Earth*.

1920s Petoskey

Ann couldn't believe she was so far from home. The farthest she had ever been before was when her mother took her to tea in Hastings for her seventh birthday. Her mother had driven them in the carriage pulled by their driving horses, Beauty and Jack.

This time, she was riding in an automobile. It was splendid, big and black and shiny with leather seats. It was marvelous to sit here next to her mother while her uncle drove. The wheels rolled underneath without any horses to make them turn. Probably the horses would have been faster, though, and not any bumpier a ride than this. Besides, horses never got flat tires that had to be changed. They had stopped once already and waited for Uncle Will to change a flat tire.

Uncle Will had taken off the side curtains after it stopped raining. The breeze ruffled her hair on this late August day, and Ann would like to stick her head out. But she was sitting in the middle.

"Cause you're small, and you fit better." Her brother grinned.

"Your father would never have ridden in an automobile." Ann's mother sat with her head up, gloved hands folded in her lap. "He loved his horses too much. He said his horses understood what he wanted them to do. You can't talk to a machine and be understood."

"Oh, Sara, now you can't beat an automobile for travelling. You see, once you crank it up, the pistons go up and down, the pistons turn the crankshaft, the crankshaft turns the drive shaft, and the drive shaft turns the axle to make the wheels go around." In the front seat, Uncle Will was explaining again how the automobile worked. He was so proud of it you'd think he had built it himself. He knew enough about automobiles that he could build one, Ann thought. Aunt Hazel sat patiently beside him, ignoring every word as she tatted the lace for which she was famous.

Ann remembered how she had once gone out in the field with her father when he drove the two big workhorses that pulled the plow. He might not like automobiles, but she sure wished he was here with them.

John began to whistle, and Ann looked over at her eleven-year-old brother. His hands rested on his basketball and his fingers tapped out a rhythm as if he were dribbling it. He took that basketball everywhere. Well, almost everywhere. His mother refused to let him take it to church.

"Are we slowing down?" Aunt Hazel stopped tatting and looked out the front window.

"Looks like it. We're not going to make it up this hill." Uncle Will stepped on the brake, and the auto stopped. "Everybody out. I'll drive up the hill, and you'll have to walk the rest of the way. Meet you at the top."

"Oh, dear." Aunt Hazel shoved her tatting into her bag. "Not again."

Ann slid out of the car and stood by her mother. She wondered if you had to rest autos like you did horses. Automobiles seemed to tire when climbing a hill.

Sunshine poured down from a clear blue sky. Ann sniffed the tangy pine air as a blue jay called. She imagined she was a princess, alighting from a royal carriage in the middle of a foreign land. Perhaps there were robbers about who would try and steal her jewels. She hugged her rag doll closer to protect her.

Her mother touched her head gently, bringing her back to reality. Reality reminded her that she looked nothing like a princess with her hair cut short. It had been cut to try and lower her fever when she was sick all those weeks with scarlet fever.

"Are you warm enough?" Her mother draped a shawl over across her shoulders.

Ann sighed. How could she be cold on such a lovely sunny day in early June? Would her mother never stop fussing about her? If her father were here, he would say, "My girl's not cold on this beautiful summer afternoon."

John jumped out and began dribbling his ball back and forth across the road. There were no other autos in sight.

"Now, John, you come over here and walk beside me. I don't want you to get all mussed up before we get there. My friend Edith runs a very ritzy resort in Petoskey, and I want us all to look nice when we arrive."

John dribbled across to her and pretended to shoot an imaginary basket behind her head. He stuck his basketball under his arm and trudged quickly up the hill, kicking the gravel on the road.

Uncle Will let the auto coast back down the hill and then backed it up to the top. The car crept along so slowly that they all reached the top of the hill before it arrived. Even Aunt Hazel was panting a bit. At the top of the hill, Ann's eyes widened. Sparkling blue water stretched out on one side of the bluff as far as she could see. "That's it! That's Lake Michigan!"

"Wow! I've never seen a lake where you can't see the other side!" John pointed toward the distance over the water. "Look at that big freighter out there."

Probably coming all the way from Chicago," said Aunt Hazel.

"Come on, everybody. Hop back in." Uncle Will stuck his arm out of the car and gestured. "Don't want to stop and have to crank this auto up again.

John jumped on the running board and held on until his mother told him to get in the car and sit down. Blue spots winked through the trees as the lake faded from view.

"There it is, at the top of that next hill." A long, elegant white building with a columned porch along the entire front sat perched on top of the hill, overlooking Lake Michigan.

At the bottom of the driveway that curved up the hill to the inn, everyone got out and walked while Uncle Will drove the car up to the hotel entrance.

A tall woman in an ankle length print dress waved to them from the porch. "Margaret, how lovely to see you. She hugged Mother and shook hands with Aunt Hazel and Uncle Will as they were introduced. "I'm so glad all of you could come. And this must be John and Ann. I haven't seen you since you were babies." She smiled at both of them.

"How do you do?" Ann smiled back at Margaret.

"How do?" John said.

"Come in, and I'll show you to your rooms. You must be tired after driving all day. Dinner will be served in the dining room at 6:00." Margaret took Mother's suitcase and led them inside and through the arched doorway to the lobby.

The setting sun through the large lakeside windows sparkled off the crystal chandeliers that hung from the high ceiling. Dark wood chairs and flowered settees sat along the walls or in clusters. They followed Margaret up the wide polished wood staircase to their rooms. Ann trailed her hand along the smooth wood banister. Margaret unlocked the door and showed Aunt Hazel and Uncle Will into their room.

"Sarah, I've put you in a room of your own."

"Oh, Margaret, it's lovely." Ann's mother smiled as she entered the room next door.

"And John and Ann, this is your room." Margaret let them into the room across the hall from their mother. "I'll leave you to unpack."

Ann walked around the room, admiring the pink velvet drapes that matched the roses in the flowered wallpaper and the plump twin beds covered with elegant matelassé spreads.

"Hey, Ann! Look at this!" John had opened the door to a small room next to the armoire.

Ann ran to see what he was so excited about. "Wow! There's a toilet and a bathtub and a sink with a faucet."

"And look." John turned the knob of the faucet, and water flowed into the sink.

"You get water right out of the tap, without pumping it." Ann stuck her fingers under the running water. "It's warm, too." She turned the golden faucet off and then on/off again.

"And, there's one to fill the tub. You can take a bath without carrying or heating water. That is, if you really wanted to take a bath."

"Do you think there's time before dinner?" Ann looked longingly at the ceramic tub sitting on sculpted legs.

"No. But look at this." John pulled the chain above the toilet and they heard a whooshing sound.

"It flushes. And, there's toilet paper." Ann touched the roll of paper beside the toilet. "This place is really luxurious. I wish we could live here instead of the farm. Imagine not going to the outhouse when it's freezing cold outside!"

"Yeah, I'd miss the animals, though. And Ma would probably make us take baths all the time."

Ann nodded. Hot baths in the bathtub without carrying and heating water didn't sound too bad.

They heard a knock on the door, and heard Mother telling them it was time to dress and come down to the dining room.

Ann put on her best dress, and John pulled on clean knickers and a shirt. At the bottom of the stairs, their mother waited for them.

The restaurant host ushered them into the dining room. The room was papered in dark red wallpaper with flecks of gold. Huge dark wood cabinets filled with beautiful dishes lined the walls. White linen tablecloths covered the tables, with gleaming white dishes set at each place. Lace curtains hung at the windows that lined three of the walls.

A waiter with a white towel draped over his arm showed them to their table by the window and pulled out a chair for each of them. Aunt Hazel and Uncle Will were already seated.

"Lovely room, isn't it." Aunt Hazel beamed at them.

"These are funny." John picked up a small bowl sitting by his plate that was filled with water. "How come they don't drink out of glasses here?"

"John. These are finger bowls to rinse your hands in." Mother shook her head. "I know we've never been to a restaurant as nice as this."

Ann sighed with pleasure as the waiter standing behind her chair set food before her and whisked it away when she was finished. She ate soup, pork chops with potatoes and gravy, vegetables, fresh slices of tomatoes, and cake and ice cream for dessert.

While the grownups talked, Ann watched the other diners. Over by the window she spotted a girl about her age sitting across from a woman who was probably her mother. Ann thought the girl's long curly red hair was beautiful. Just then, the girl looked up and smiled at Ann. Ann smiled back. She would like to get to know that girl.

After dinner, Ann soaked in the bathtub as long as her mother allowed. She dried off with one of the thick white towels, put on her nightgown and climbed into the high, soft bed. After the long day, she fell asleep quickly.

The next morning, after a breakfast of pancakes, eggs, and toast, Ann sat in a rocking chair on the porch beside her mother. She wanted to ask her mother if they could somehow get down to the water of Lake Michigan, which looked so close but seemed out of reach. But her mother was talking with Aunt Hazel and Margaret. Ann knew her mother would not want to be interrupted.

"Hey, Ma," John hopped onto the porch, his basketball tucked under his arm. "Can I go to the play yard at the school with Bob, the cook's son? He says there's a basketball hoop there." John nodded to the boy who stood beside him and gave his mother his most winning smile. "Please."

"May I go," his mother corrected. "I guess it's okay. But it's not polite to interrupt an adult conversation."

"Sorry, ma'am." John dashed off after his new friend.

Ann saw the girl with the curly golden red hair at the other end of the porch. The girl looked up and waved. Ann rose from her chair and walked to the end of the porch.

"Hello, I'm Ann."

"Hello back. I'm Betsy. What's your doll's name?"

"Jane. She's named after my best friend from school."

"I have a doll, but I didn't bring her. My mother said I can go downtown to the dime store, if I want. I have my own money." She showed Ann the purse she was carrying. "Do you want to come?"

Ann nodded. She patted her pocked where she kept the change purse with the dollar she had received from Uncle Will. "Do you know the way?"

"Yes. My mother brings me here from Chicago every August, because I have hay fever and I'm better up here."

"All the way from Chicago. And you get to stay in this grand hotel every summer."

"It's not so grand. There's usually no one to play with. So, can you go downtown?"

"Come on. I'll ask my mother." She led the way to the other end of the porch.

"Mom, this is Betsy. She's going downtown. Can I, may I go?"

Her mother looked up. "Hello. I don't know, dear. How far is it?'

"It's fine," said Margaret. "Betsy comes here every summer. She knows her way downtown. They're perfectly safe."

"Well, okay then."

"Thanks." Ann handed her mother the doll. She and Betsy raced down the steps and across the lawn to the path that led to town.

They crossed a little bridge over a narrow creek and walked down the hill into town. Stores on either side of the street offered enticing things. They passed a hat shop, a dress shop, the hardware store, a drug store, and an ice cream shop.

"We can come back here after the dime store." Betsy pointed to the sign shaped like a strawberry ice cream cone that hung over the door. Ann glanced in at the round tables and red and white striped chairs. On the farm, they had homemade ice cream, but she loved to order a sundae at an ice cream shop.

Betsy pushed open the door of the dime store and led Ann to the candy counter. They walked along the counter looking at the displays of candy: lemon drops, chocolate drops, peanut clusters, peppermint sticks, spearmint gum.

"I like these." Betsy pointed to the chocolate drops. "What's your favorite?"

"I like them all, but I think I like the lemon drops best."

"May I help you?" A young sales woman smiled at them from behind the counter.

"I'll treat," said Betsy. "We'd like two pennies' worth of lemon drops and two pennies' worth of chocolate drops."

The sales clerk opened the backs of the cases, scooped up the candy, and weighed it on a scale. She dumped the candy into a small white bag and handed it to Betsy.

Sucking on chocolate drops and lemon drops, Ann and Betsy wandered up and down the aisles looking at all the treasures. They admired the shelf of ceramic dolls and doll clothes, tried on charm bracelets, and leafed through the shelf of books.

As they walked around the store, Ann stopped at a counter of wooden toys. "Boats. We could sail boats in the bathtub."

Betsy picked up one of the red wooden boats with small white sails. "We could. I've never tried that."

Ann picked up several boats and examined them before she chose a blue boat with a striped sail. She handed the dollar to the clerk and carefully counted the change she received.

At the ice cream store, they sat at one of the tables and ordered strawberry sundaes. The ice cream felt smooth and creamy on their tongues, and the strawberries tasted sweet and syrupy.

When they entered the hotel, Ann heard her mother's voice in the parlor, talking with Aunt Hazel. Ann and Betsy rushed up the stairs to Ann's room. Ann turned on the golden faucet and filled the bathtub with three inches of water. She and Betsy unbuttoned their shoes and took them off. They stepped into the tub and pushed their boats back and forth. Ann splashed the water and watched the boats bob up and down on the waves. Betsy laughed as Ann turned on the faucet and sailed the boats under the waterfall. By dinner time their dresses were damp, and they had to change before going down to the dining room.

After dinner, Betsy and Ann were outside on the porch when John passed them as he went down the steps. "Where are you going? Does Mom know you're leaving the porch?" Ann was sure he was going somewhere interesting.

"Mom doesn't have to know everything. If you promise not to tell, you can come."

Ann looked at Betsy, and Betsy nodded. "Okay."

"Come on, then." John walked off across the lawn, and Ann and Betsy followed.

"Where are we going?" Ann asked when they caught up.

"To Lake Michigan. Bob knows a place where you can find those old dinosaur stones with the spots on them."

"I know about those," said Betsy, "but my mother would never let me go to the beach alone, and she doesn't like me to be near the water."

"Well, I'm going to find a ton of them," John boasted.

"Me, too," said Ann.

Bob met them at the bottom of the hill and led them across the road and down the steep embankment to the Lake. Ann and Betsy raced down to the beach that edged the shoreline. Small waves rolled in with a steady rhythm. Swish, swish. The sun sat low in the sky, and faint swirls of pink fanned around it. The lake had lost its brilliant blue and turned darker. Ann stared. The lake was so big and extended out to forever.

John and Bob had already kicked off their shoes and were running down the beach, dodging the waves. Ann and Betsy unbuttoned their shoes and set them carefully away from the waves.

"What are we looking for?" Ann called to the boys, as she and Betsy ran after them.

The boys stopped running and searched the edge of the water for stones.

"What do the dinosaur stones look like?" Ann looked at all the different shapes and sizes of stones along the shore.

"They're not really dinosaur stones," said Bob. "They're from the coral that used to be here a long, long time ago, millions of years. When the glaciers melted, they dropped them all over the place. Now they're fossils. There are lots of them around here."

"Oh," said Ann. "But how do you know when you've found one?"

"They're about the size of a small potato, round and smooth and gray with dark hexagon-shaped spots. They show up best when they're wet." Bob and John walked off down the beach.

Ann and Betsy walked slowly along the edge of the water, picking up stones and tossing them back. Ann nudged the tip of a stone with her toe, kneeled down, and dug it out of the sand.

"Do you think this is it?" She held it out to Betsy,

"Maybe."

Ann put it in her pocket and kept looking. When they again caught up with the boys, Bob was showing John how to skip stones out across the water. Ann counted as Bob's stone hopped six times.

"I wish I could do that," said Ann.

"Girls can't skip stones." John held his arm back and his stone hopped once before plopping in the water.

Ann took the stone she had found out of her pocket and held it out for Bob to see. It was round and smooth, about the size of one of the first small potatoes dug in the fall. "Do you think this is one of those fossils?"

Bob whistled. "Hey, that's a big one."

"Really? Is it real?"

"Yup."

"Just dumb luck." John frowned.

"We can share it." Ann looked intently at the stone and put it back in her pocket.

She looked at Betsy. "But you didn't find one."

"I don't mind. This is the first time I've been down by the water barefoot." Betsy grinned and scrunched her toes in the wet sand.

"So, have you seen the ghost yet?" Bob skipped another stone across the water.

"What ghost?" Ann had never seen a ghost. Were they even real?

"The ghost at the Inn. Lots of people have seen it or heard it."

"What kind of ghost? Never seen one. You?"

"I haven't seen it, but people say sometimes when they are walking down the hallway, they see the shadowy ghost of a man walking towards them. Or maybe a door just slams on its own. Some people have even heard the piano playing when there was no one sitting at it."

"You're just trying to scare us." Betsy put her hands on her hips.

"Nope. True stories."

The sun now looked like a big, golden ball falling slowly into the water. Pink, orange and yellow streaks spread across the sky.

"Hey, we better get back. Mom will have a fit, if she finds we're not around the hotel and it's dark." She turned and called to her brother. "John, come on!"

Ann grabbed Betsy's hand as they dashed back down the beach. They climbed the sand dune back up to the road, giggling as they slid backwards through the soft sand. Brushing the sand off their feet, they rebuttoned their shoes and hurried back to the hotel.

"Betsy, is that you? Where have you been?"

Betsy turned toward the voice at the end of the porch. She squeezed Ann's hand. "See you tomorrow."

Ann's mother sat on the porch with Aunt Hazel, Uncle Will, and Margaret, watching the sunset. She narrowed her eyes and looked at Ann and John as they ran up onto the porch.

"Where have you two been all this time?"

"Bottom of the hill. Watching the sunset." John grinned. That was true, Ann thought. The sand dune hill.

Her mother looked at the wet hem of Ann's dress. "Must be a bit damp down there."

"Early dew, I expect," said Margaret.

"Look what I found." Ann held out her hand that held the Petoskey stone.

"That is the real thing. And a big one at that." Margaret smiled at Ann and Ann smiled back.

Margaret turned to Ann's mother. "Petoskey stones are a special find around here. Fossils from long ago."

"Lucky you." Her Mother smiled. "A nice reminder of our trip. Well, you'd better get ready for bed now. "I'll come and say goodnight."

Upstairs, Ann put on her best nightgown and gazed out the window. The sky looked as if a strawberry milkshake had been splashed across the blue, as the last of the sun slipped under the horizon. She hugged the stuffed bear that she always took to bed and snuggled underneath the covers. She felt the smooth coolness of the Petoskey stone in her hand.

Their mother came in and kissed them both.

"Goodnight. Sleep right."

"Goodnight, Mama." Their mother quietly left.

Suddenly, a door slammed with a loud thud.

"Was that the ghost?" Ann whispered.

"Probably. Bob said it does that sometimes."

Ann shivered and snuggled down into the covers.

"John, do you think we'll see the ghost?"

"Probably not. But I don't want to miss it, so if you see it, let me know."

Ann sighed. "Hasn't this been the best vacation ever?"
"Yeah." John mumbled and rolled over.

Early the next morning, Ann and Betsy sat on the porch step.

"Will you come back next summer?" Betsy looked at Ann.

"I don't know. I hope so."

"Maybe you'll come to Chicago."

"Or you might come to Hastings." Ann looked hopeful.

"We'll always be friends. I'll write to you."

"Let's get some paper, so I can give you my address."

At the front desk, the clerk handed them each a piece of hotel stationary and a pencil. Back on the porch, they wrote down their addresses and exchanged papers.

"I'll write to you as soon as you leave," promised Betsy.

"And I'll write back as soon as I get it."

Her mother, Aunt Hazel, Uncle Will and Margaret came out on the porch with a porter carrying their luggage. Margaret hugged her mother.

"Oh, Sara, I do hope you can come back. It was so lovely to see you again."

"I will if I can. And you're always welcome to visit us in Hastings." She looked across the lawn to where John and Bob played catch.

"Time to go, John."

John looked up. He punched Bob lightly on the arm, and Bob grinned. "See you sometime."

Everyone said goodbye, and Ann and her family climbed back into Uncle Will's car. As they drove down the hill, Ann turned and watched out the back window as the hotel grew smaller in the distance. She made a wish on the Petoskey stone that they would come back someday.

FUN FACTS:

Where is Petoskey?

Petoskey is a town in northwestern Michigan on the shore of Lake Michigan. The Odawa, Indigenous people in Northern Michigan, call this land "Wahanakising" which means

"Land of the Crooked Tree." Crooked trees were used to mark significant locations, or to signify Odawa homelands. In 1715, the French settled in the area and translated the name to "L'Arbre Croche." Later, the city was named Petoskey after Ottawa Chief Ignatius Petoskey. His Indigenous name was Bidassige, or Pe-to-se-ga, which is said to mean "The Rising Sun."

(www.petoskeydowntown.com)

What kind of cars were available in the 1920s?

Cars popular in the 1920s included a 1929 Ford Deluxe Roadster, 1920 Rolls-Royce Phantom Limousine, 1926 Packard Twin 6 Roadster, 1920 Nash Touring, and a 1929 Studebaker Roadster. In 1921, 61 percent of the cars sold were Ford Model T's.

(The Greatest Cars of the 1920s, on Celebrating Iconic Cars: supercars.net)

Aloha

Gavin grabbed his suitcase and his sister's suitcase off the carousel in Baggage Claim and carried them over to where his sister Arianna and his mother waited.

"Thanks." Arianna took her suitcase and placed the handles of her tote over the suitcase handle. They watched as Dad grabbed his suitcase and then pulled Mom's suitcase off as it came around on the carousel.

The four of them wheeled their cases out of the airport into the sunshine.

"Wow, blue sky and sunshine. Haven't seen that for a while." Arianna turned her face to the sun.

"Hawaii in January is pretty cool, or warm." Gavin smiled and looked around. "But it's all covered in black stone. I thought Hawaii was tropical trees and flowers."

"That's lava. We'll see the tropical side of the island, but there are several volcanoes here that have been active on and off for years. The air smells great, though." Mom breathed deeply.

"Didn't expect all this lava, but it's an adventure to see what it's like. I've read about volcanoes, but I never knew they covered so much area with lava. Let's pick up the rental car and drive to our rental house. Wonder what the rest of the island looks like." Dad led the way to the car lot.

They found their car, stowed the luggage, and settled in. The one road around the island passed through more land covered in lava.

"We should check out that beach, maybe." Arianna pointed to a sign for White Sands Beach Park on the side of the road.

"And Kahaluʻu Beach Park." Gavin pointed to the next sign.

"There's Greenwell Coffee Farm. We should check that out." Dad smiled. "Kona coffee is supposed to be some of the best."

"There's a monument to Captain Cook. I guess he explored here a lot," said Gavin.

"After he introduced the world to Hawaii, he died here," said Mom. "Was that the road we're looking for that we just passed?" Mom pointed behind them.

"Oops. It was hard to spot." Dad turned the car around and turned down a two-track road lined with trees and flowering bushes on both sides. "This looks more tropical." The car bumped down the road a bit further and then the road ended. "Looks like we have arrived."

A tall, older, fit-looking woman stepped out from the trees. "Aloha. You are staying with us?"

"That's us," said Mom.

"I am your hostess, Barbara. Your house is just through here. Follow me. Need help with your luggage?"

"We've got it. Thanks. Lead the way." The family followed her down a path to an Asian style house, set in a huge garden filled with trees and flowers. Arianna spied an orange tree and a lemon tree as they walked past.

A white cat sat on the front steps. His blue eyes stared curiously at them.

"This is Pueo. He likes to greet the guests. You will probably see him a lot, as he is fond of people. The other cats who live at my house next door are a bit skittish, so you may not often see them."

Arianna and Gavin both stopped to pet Pueo. He rubbed against them and purred.

"You are welcome to visit us anytime, Pueo. I miss our cat back home." Arianna rubbed underneath his chin.

"This is the kitchen." Barbara gestured to the appliances and table and chairs in the room across the front of the house. "Back here is the master bedroom and sitting area. You can leave your luggage here, and I will show you the other buildings where there are two more bedrooms, the bathroom, and shower."

Gavin looked at Arianna and she raised her eyebrows. Sounded like an interesting arrangement.

Barbara took them around to the back of the house, where they climbed an outside stairway. At the top of the stairs, they entered another bedroom with a bed next to the wall, a small table and chair, and a sitting area with two chairs. Then she led them back down the stairs to a building across the walkway to the house. She showed them the bathroom and an outdoor shower room, open to the sky with a shower curtain across the front. They climbed another outdoor stairway that led to a bedroom similar to the one they had just seen.

"Well, I'll let you get settled in. If you have any questions, just come on over and give me a shout."

"One question. We passed a small grocery store but did not stop for groceries yet. Is there a good place to eat dinner nearby?"

"I would recommend the Hotel Manago. It is just down the road, about a half-mile from where you turned in here."

After Barbara left, the family explored the house where they would be staying for the week.

"I'll take the bedroom across from the main house," Arianna said. She looked at Gavin. "Are you okay with the room upstairs at the back of the house?"

"Sure. I'll go put my things in there."

After getting settled in, they got back into the car and drove to the Manago. The inside had dark wood floors and paneling on the walls. Tables with brightly colored chairs filled the space.

"What is opakapaka? Or 'opelu?" Gavin looked up from his menu.

"That's a good question. We'll ask our server when she comes back."

The server brought water and asked them if they had any questions about the menu. She told them that opakapaka was the Hawaiian name for pink snapper and 'opelu the name of mackerel.

"I'll have the opakapaka," said Dad.

"I'll have the same," said Mom.

Gavin chose hamburger steak and Arianna the teri chicken.

When their meals came, they included three sides: black-eyed peas, succotash, and potato/macaroni salad.

"Interesting side dishes," said Gavin, "but it all tastes good."

After dinner, they stocked up on groceries and returned to their rental house. Arianna helped put away the food and then went outside to explore the gardens. She took pictures of the tropical flowers that she did not know the names of.

In the morning, Arianna yawned as she came into the kitchen, yawning. "Those silly roosters started crowing while it was still dark. I thought they were supposed to wake people up at the beginning of the day."

"Did they wake you up? I must have slept right through it," said Dad.

"They were right outside my bedroom window."

"Glad I slept in the back then," said Gavin.

"Barbara said they belong to a neighbor, and they like to come over and visit.," said Mom. "Sorry they woke you up."

"Maybe I'll get used to them."

On the drive to Volcano National Park they saw fields of lava extending as far as they could see, with a two-foot wall of black lava along the road.

At the Visitor Center, Arianna pointed to a large display of the five volcanoes on Hawaii island. "Imagine living where there are five volcanoes. Mauna Loa and Kilauea still erupt sometimes, but Mauna Kea hasn't erupted for 5,000 years."

Gavin read from a sign by the display. "It says here that Kilauea, which is really Halema'uma'u in Hawaiian, is the home of the Goddess Pele. She is the ruler of volcanoes, and people sometimes still offer her tributes."

"I'm going to buy that postcard with her pictures."

Along the trail to the volcano, they spotted several steam vents created by slits in the rock a distance from Kilauea. From the lookout platform, they could see the rim of the volcano. Smoke rose up from the center of it.

"If we had been here a few months ago, we might have seen it erupting. The video at the Visitor Center was amazing, how the volcano spewed out lava, then filled up with water, then the water evaporated, and it spewed out lava again."

"I wish we could have seen it erupting, but we might not have been able to get very close because of the chemicals that are bad to breathe."

"That's true."

Before leaving the park, they ate at Volcano House Hotel, which dated back to 1846 and was recently restored. They sat at a table by the window and looked out at the rim of Halema'uma'u.

"I think I'll be adventurous and try the Hawaiian food plate," Gavin said. "

"I will, too. We should try everything while we're here." Arianna nodded. "What is poke, though?"

"I looked it up. It's raw fish, a Hawaiian favorite."

"I'll be glad to donate my poke to someone then," Arianna said.

Their parents also chose to try the food plate which consisted of fish, poke, poi, potato/macaroni salad, steamed rice, and salad.

On their way to Hapuna Beach, they stopped in Kailua-Kona and shopped for Aloha shirts. Gavin bought a dark blue one with white flowers and Arianna bought a red one with pale yellow flowers.

"That looks good on you." Arianna nodded to Gavin, who had put on his shirt when he got back to the car. "I didn't think you'd be brave enough to wear an aloha shirt with flowers on it."

"When in Hawaii, you have to wear an aloha shirt." Gavin grinned.

"Would you wear it at home?"

"Probably not."

The parking area at the beach was full of cars, and they drove around for a couple of minutes until their mom spotted a parking space. They already wore their bathing suits, so they just walked down to the beach.

"Wow! This is the real Hawaii." Arianna gazed down the long beach that stretched from one set of cliffs to another at the other end. Gentle waves lapped the shore of the clean, white sand. Arianna and Gavin spread out their towels, slipped off their sandals, and walked down to the water. They gave each other a daring look, and both raced in and dove under.

"Feels great! Not too cold."

Later, they walked along the hard-packed sand to the far end of the beach and back. Even though the parking lot was full, the beach did not feel crowded.

As they drove back toward their house, they saw the sign for Puʻuhonua o Hōnaunau National Historic Park.

"We should stop there," said Mom. "When Kamehameha was king, it was set up as a sanctuary where anyone could seek refuge."

"Anyone? Like who?" asked Gavin.

"Someone who had broken the law could seek forgiveness, or families of combatants, or defeated warriors."

"Interesting idea," said Dad.

Inside the park they saw structures where people lived, the king's compound, and an outdoor concrete table and chairs where people played board games.

When Gavin came down to breakfast in the morning, Mom was making coffee and buttering toast, and Dad was cooking eggs. On the porch, Arianna looked in the wooden box where their hostess left fresh fruit she had picked from the garden.

"Hey, look at these." Coming back into the kitchen, Arianna held up two fruits. One of them was orangish in color and in the shape of an egg, but much larger. The other was yellow with blunt spikes sticking out.

"That first one might be an eggfruit. Our hostess said they are ripe right now," said Mom.

"That other one is a dragon fruit," said Gavin.

"How did you know that?"

"I saw a picture of one somewhere. Open them up, and let's see how they taste."

Arianna sliced each of them in half. "Looks like we're supposed to scoop the fruit out with a spoon, maybe." She handed half of the dragon fruit to Gavin and half to her parents. She kept half of the eggfruit and handed half to her parents as well. She spooned out a bite from the eggfruit. "This tastes like a combination of a sweet potato and an orange. It's good." She passed it to Gavin, who tasted it and nodded in agreement.

Gavin scooped out a spoonful from the dragon fruit. "Yum. Tastes a lot like honeydew." He handed the half to Arianna.

"I agree. Wish we had more of these."

While they ate breakfast, they talked about what to do for the day.

"Let's go to Punalu'u Black Sand Beach. I want to see the green turtles that are supposed to hang out there," said Arianna.

Gavin looked at the map of Hawaii. "After that, we could drive all the way to Hilo. We haven't seen that side of the island. It's supposed to rain more over there than it does on this side."

"Sounds like a plan. We'd better get ourselves ready. Driving always takes a while with just one two-lane road around the island." Dad got up and started carrying dishes to the sink.

"The beach is, well, black. Just like the guidebook said it would be," Gavin said when they arrived at the beach.

"Look at all those turtles. They're so big! And there are lots of them. But they look so dried out, and their eyes are closed." Arianna got out her camera.

"Look, there's one coming out of the water up onto the beach."

Arianna zoomed in the camera and took a picture. Just then, one of them opened its eye and blinked at her. "Hey, I think that one just winked at me."

"Sure," said Gavin. "Probably likes his picture taken."

As they drove on to Hilo, it rained for the first time since they had arrived in Hawaii. Stands at the flea market in the main part of town sold produce and other Hawaiian items. The clerk at the locavore store gave them a free eggfruit because it was ripe. From a small store on the main street, Mom bought a pink scarf with flowers

On their drive back to the rental house, they turned off the highway, drove to the most southern point of the island, and ate at the southernmost restaurant. When they returned to the house, Pueo was sitting on the porch.

"Hi, Pueo. Did you stop by for a treat?" Arianna let him inside and fed him a couple of the treats that Barbara had left for them to give him. He ate the treat quickly, then curled up on the bed and went to sleep.

"Looks like he feels right at home." Gavin laughed.

"Since we saw the most southern point of the island, tomorrow we should visit the most northern point of the island."

"Sure, why not?" said Dad.

The next morning, they drove north, passing through Kailua-Kona. As usual, there was a lot of traffic on the only road around the island. As they traveled farther north, they saw less traffic and the terrain changed. The houses looked more like what they were used to at home, with grass lawns instead of lava. Halawa Keokea Beach Park included scenic cliffs and a rocky shoreline.

"Doesn't look like a swimming area. Too many rocks and really big surf," Gavin said.

"I like it, though. It's different from the other parts of the island," said Mom.

"That's the birthplace of King Kamehameha I." Gavin pointed to the sign on the side of the road as they drove back toward their house. "After him, there were Kamehameha II and Kamehameha III."

"There was one queen, though. Lili'uokalani. She didn't get to rule very long, but she is remembered because she tried to defend Hawaii from being taken by the United States," Arianna said.

To please Dad, they stopped at the Greenwell Coffee Farm that they had passed and learned all about coffee.

"Some of the trees on our farm are 100 years old. We pick the cherries by hand and take off the skins. Then we dry the beans and take the outer husks off." The tour guide gestured to the people who raked the large trays of beans to dry them. He held out his hand to show them the green coffee bean that was underneath the husk.

Back at the entrance, they sampled the different coffees, and Dad chose a bag of Kona coffee beans to take home. Arianna and her mom admired the flowers growing on the farm.

"That's ʻōhiʻa lehua, the flower of the state tree." Mom pointed at a red flower.

"Beautiful orchids," said Arianna.

"Tomorrow is the next-to-the-last day before we go home. What shall we do?" Mom looked at Arianna and Gavin.

"Green Sands Beach," they both said together.

"It's supposed to be green because of a mineral called olivine that was in the lava that created the beach," said Gavin.

"This is probably the only time we'll ever see a green beach," said Arianna.

In the morning they drove down a dirt road to the parking lot for Green Sand Beach. Mom parked the car and they all got out. People walked down a rutted dirt road, and they followed them down to the ocean.

"Looks like the path we want starts over there." Dad pointed to a path to the left.

The trail area was open and stark, without trees or much greenery. Views of the water were spectacular, as big surf splashed against the rocky shore. The path seemed to go on and on in the distance.

"How far did you say it was to Green Sand Beach?"

"Six miles roundtrip."

Arianna and Gavin walked along briskly, in a hurry to get to the beach. They had their swimsuits on under their clothes and were eager to get into the water.

"You two walk as fast as you want. If you get ahead of us, we'll catch up with you," Dad called to them.

"Do you think it will be really green?" said Gavin.

"I hope it's, like, bright green or lime green. That would be way cool."

"I hope so, too."

They felt they had walked a long way already, and they could see their parents far in the distance behind them. Suddenly, they stopped. Trails seemed to go in many directions.

"Which way, do you think? They all look like they go to the same place, but maybe not."

Gavin squinted up ahead and pointed. "I think on the other side of that bluff I can see what looks like a bay. Let's just keep going on this trail. It looks like they all go in that general direction."

Arianna nodded, and they kept walking.

Finally, they could see people walking down toward the water. They had arrived at the beach.

"That's disappointing. It looks more brownish-green than bright green."

"True. Oh, well. At least we can go swimming. We should wait for Mom and Dad, though, so they'll know where we are." They shrugged out of their backpacks and spread out their towels to sit on. Arianna leaned back and closed her eyes.

"Wake up. Mom and Dad are here. Let's go in."

Arianna sat up. "Hi, you made it. We're going in."

"Okay. Don't go out too far, and be careful."

"Course."

Arianna and Gavin waded out into the water and plunged in. Arianna began to swim to get past all the people standing around in the water. She looked back to make sure that Gavin was with her.

"Yikes! What was that?" Arianna shrieked.

"What's wrong?" Gavin called over to her.

"Something bumped me underneath. There aren't sharks out here, are there? Maybe we should swim back." Just then, a head appeared above the water and a large shell emerged behind it. She looked into the eyes of a green turtle.

"Hey, something bumped me, too." Gavin yelled. "Maybe we should get out of here!"

"It's turtles," Arianna yelled back. "Beautiful green turtles!" Three green turtles swam past her, not close enough to touch her.

Underneath her, she felt a gentle touch. As the turtle rose up to the surface, its shell was underneath her, and she was being pulled along. For a moment, she panicked, thinking it might pull her out to sea. Then it slowly turned and swam in a large circle. Holding on tightly, she felt the hard shell under her hands, the flap of the turtle's feet as it swam.

"Wow! Look at me!"

Arianna laughed as Gavin held on to another turtle that swam in circles, going in the opposite direction she was going. Other turtles swam slowly around them, making little ripples in the water. She wondered if her parents could see them. What would they think?

After a few minutes, her turtle slipped quietly under the water, and she let go of its shell. It surfaced next to her and blinked one eye. Gavin's turtle, too, had slipped away. All the turtles sank slowly under the water. Suddenly, they could no longer see any of the turtles. Then, farther out in the ocean, they saw them swimming away.

"We'd better swim back to shore." Gavin swam up beside her. "How cool was that?"

"That was amazing! I wonder if anyone noticed we were swimming with turtles." Arianna swam slowly behind Gavin back toward shore.

When they got close enough to shore that they could no longer swim without touching the bottom, they stood up. "There's Dad on shore looking for us in the water." Gavin gestured with his head.

"We weren't very far out, and we're good swimmers."

"Hope he sees it that way."

They trotted out of the water and walked up to where their dad stood.

"The water is great, not even cold. You should go in." Arianna smiled at her dad.

"I was trying to keep track of you, but you were pretty far out. Looked like some kind of creature out there, and I was worried."

"It wasn't that deep. There were some turtles out there, though, and we got to see them up close." Arianna smiled.

"Real close," said Gavin.

"Well, that sounds like an adventure. Next time, stay closer, though. This is the ocean, you know."

"Okay." Gavin and Arianna nodded.

The next day, they were all quiet as they packed their bags for the trip home.

"We have to come back again. I love Hawaii." Arianna looked out the window at the gardens of fruit and flowers.

"Me, too," said Gavin.

Arianna and Gavin sat on the back porch and petted Pueo.

"Thanks for being such a great host, Pueo."

"I will tell our cat Fuzzy all about you."

Barbara came to say goodbye, as they loaded their luggage into the car. She held Pueo and waved as they drove away.

FUN FACTS:

What makes green turtles green?

Green sea turtles are the largest of the hard-shelled turtles. They eat mostly seagrasses and algae, and this is what makes them a greenish color. Their shells are dark brown, gray, or olive colored. Adults can grow three to four feet long, weigh 250-400 pounds, and live up to 70 years.

Because green sea turtles have been used for their fat, meat and eggs, their numbers have declined. The United States and other countries prohibit killing them or collecting their eggs.

(fisheries.noaa.gov/species/green-turtle)

Who were the original people in Hawaii?

The first people to arrive in Hawaii sailed from Polynesia in double-hulled canoes. They crossed 2,400 miles of open ocean navigating by the sun and stars and reading winds, currents, and the flight of seabirds. Later, Polynesians arrived from the Society Islands and became the new rulers. During 400 years of isolation from the rest of the world, Hawaiians developed their own unique culture. They fished; raised pigs, dogs and chickens; and harvested sweet potatoes, taro, and other crops. They worshiped their own gods and created their own songs and dance (hula). Today, many Hawaiians still treasure their culture and language.

(nps.gov, The First Hawaiians)

What does Aloha mean in Hawaiian?

The word includes many things: respect and love for one another, kindness, and living in harmony with everything around you.

A Superior Vacation

Pine needles crunched under Lindsay's feet as she trudged along the path through the woods. The strap of her backpack cut into her shoulder, and the new hiking boots her dad had given her rubbed against her ankles.

Ahead on the path, Dad's blue jacket blinked through the trees. His sleeping bag swung back and forth on the back of his pack, and notes of his whistling drifted back to her. She didn't know what was he so cheerful about. Backpacking is just plain hard work!

She glimpsed her brother Logan's red hat up ahead, as he kept up a brisk pace behind their dad. She didn't know how she and Logan could be twins. They looked alike, tall, with green eyes like their dad, and brown, curly hair like their mom. But they certainly didn't think alike. Logan always did his best to be cheerful whenever their dad came around.

Lindsay looked down at the path and concentrated on putting one foot in front of another. She would like to stop and rest, but it hadn't been long since the last time they stopped to rest.

We should be in school anyway, she thought. It was a Friday in mid-October and a school day. Her mother had never let them miss a day of seventh grade unless they were practically dying. It was too hard to make up all the homework. But Dad had come breezing into town after not calling for the past four months and wanted to take them backpacking. To see the fall colors, he said.

Mom told him he couldn't just stop by whenever he wanted and take them out of school. Dad said it would do them good to get out in nature. Lindsay hated it when they argued. But Logan begged Mom to let them go, and she finally gave in. After all, they need to spend more time with their dad, she said.

Lindsay really didn't see the point. After the weekend of backpacking, Dad would just disappear for another four months. Logan, of course, always believed that this time Dad would stick around.

Logan hiked along behind his dad. He was happy to miss a day of school and go backpacking instead. Also, he figured if Dad saw how much fun it would be to spend time with him and his sister, he would come around more often. If only

Lindsay could see that and stop acting so mad at their dad all the time.

The canopy of tree branches overhead blocked out the thin October sunshine, darkening the path ahead. Pine boughs sighed in the wind, and a blue jay squawked as it burst upward. To Lindsay's right, flashes of blue from Lake Superior splashed through the leaves.

Lindsay hiked down the slope and up a long hill where Dad waited for her, while Logan walked on ahead. Just off the cliff on her right, sapphire blue stretched as far as she could see. Sunlight winked like gems across the gently rolling waves. In the distance, rocks cut by wind erosion formed a small castle standing high above the water. Sinking lower in the sky, the sun washed the rock castle in gold. October's days were getting shorter. *The sun still has the Midas touch,* she thought, remembering a fable they'd read in fourth grade.

"Not bad, huh? That's Chapel Rock."

"It looks like a castle to me." Lindsay sighed.

"Tired?" Dad watched her closely.

Lindsay shrugged.

"Just a little farther before we set up camp. Wait until you see the campsite."

"Hey, come on. Let's go." Logan waved to them from ahead on the trail. Maybe after they set up camp Lindsay would cheer up.

Lindsay followed her dad down the trail. The endless blue of the water disappeared behind the trees. Her pack got heavier and her feet hurt more as they followed the trail back into the trees.

At the top of a small hill, an arch carved out of the rocks stood at the edge of the trail. Wow! That was pretty cool. Lindsay walked within an arm's reach of it. She reached out and laid her hand on the rough, cool stone.

"Over here," Dad called. He slung his pack onto the ground underneath a grove of pine trees. Behind him, just ten feet away, stretched a beach of clean white sand with waves gently lapping the shore. Lindsay had to admit the beach was beautiful.

Logan's pack already lay on the ground next to his dad's. Kicking off his shoes and socks, he raced along the beach, dodging the waves. "Wow! That's cold!" he whooped.

Lindsay trudged down the hill, slung her pack down, and shrugged her shoulders to ease her muscles. She sat on the ground, pulled off her boots and wiggled her toes. Behind them, the golden castle gleamed in the setting sun.

"Not much time to rest. Got to set up camp before dark. The evenings aren't so long up here in the Upper Peninsula in October."

Dad untied his sleeping bag and the tent from his backpack. He unrolled the tent and laid it out flat. "This looks like a good flat spot. A couple of tree roots, but we'll have to try to avoid sleeping on them."

He looked down the beach. "Hey, Logan, we need some firewood." Logan slid in his tracks, turned, and raced back toward them.

Lindsay sighed. A hot shower, a pepperoni pizza, and a soda would be perfect about now.

Dad set up the tent. Logan collected firewood and dropped an armful of sticks by the fire pit. Lindsay spread out three sleeping bags inside the tent, while their dad fired up the little cookstove. She wondered how he was going to fix dinner with one little stove like that.

Whistling, he poured macaroni into boiling water. When it was al dente, he dumped out the water, stirred in a can of tomato sauce, and sprinkled seasoning from a plastic Parmesan cheese shaker. Sitting on the ground, they scooped up pasta from tin plates and nibbled dried fruit for dessert.

"Hey," said Logan, "this is the best pasta I ever had."

Lindsay rolled her eyes. "Yeah, the best."

"Come on, you love pasta, same as me. And there's nothing like eating in the great outdoors to give me an appetite." Logan took another bite of pasta.

Lindsay shook her head, but smiled. "Everything gives you an appetite."

Logan grinned.

Dad laughed. "Well, you can't expect gourmet cooking on a backpacking trip. Still, I think it hit the spot pretty well."

When the campsite was cleaned up, Dad hung the rest of the food in a bag in a tree. "Don't want to tempt those bears."

"Bears?" Lindsay looked over her shoulder at the lengthening shadows.

Dad laughed and laid another log on the fire. The three of them sat cross-legged on the ground and watched the flames shoot higher.

"We need a good ghost story," said Logan. "Come on, Dad, you must know a good story."

"Let me think." Dad leaned forward. "Yeah, I think I do. This is a great ghost story. Because it's true. And it happened right here."

"A long time ago, before the Anishinaabek came to live here, there was another tribe that flourished. They were tall and strong, with shining black hair and green eyes."

"Green eyes?" Lindsay asked skeptically.

"That's right."

"Uh huh."

"They lived in the woods near here, and that castle on the hill was their sacred place." Dad pointed to Chapel Rock, which loomed in the distance. With the sun going down, it looked dark instead of golden. "The chief had a daughter named SheWhoSparkles."

"SheWhoSparkles?" Logan said.

Dad shrugged. "That's right. She was the light of his life, and he wanted her to marry his best friend's son, whose name was HeWhoIsStrongAndBrave."

"What did her mom want?" Lindsay said.

Dad paused. "HeWhoIsStrongAndBrave's mom was her mother's best friend, so she wanted that, too."

"What about what SheWhoSparkles wanted?" Lindsay persisted.

"She loved him, I'm sure."

"How come in stories they always have to get married?" said Logan.

"That's just how life goes." Dad smiled.

"Sometimes it doesn't last too long, though, does it?" Lindsay looked straight at her dad.

"No, sometimes it doesn't work out. Anyway, the daughter loved this boy, but she had never been outside the tribe, and she wanted to have an adventure before she settled down."

"Like shooting the falls in a canoe or discovering something?" Logan asked.

"Maybe like that. Anyway, the night before the wedding, she sneaked out of the tepee when the full moon shone over the lake and pushed a canoe out onto the smooth water. You see, there was a legend that somewhere out there was an island where every day it was warm and sunny, beautiful flowers grew everywhere, and there was fruit hanging from the trees year around."

"Kind of like the Caribbean," said Lindsay.

"Right. But a great storm came up and SheWhoSparkles did not return. In the morning, HeWhoIsStrongAndBrave found that a canoe was missing and suspected that SheWho-Sparkles had taken it. Day after day he set out in his canoe, but she was never found. They say that on a night with a full moon ..."

"Like tonight." Logan pointed up at the sky.

"Like tonight. On a night with a full moon, you can hear him calling to her as he walks up and down the beach. And she comes out of the water and takes his hand."

"What happens after she takes his hand?" Lindsay rolled her eyes.

"They walk along the beach and enjoy being together."

"Maybe we'll see her tonight, then." Logan grinned.

"Right." Lindsay gazed out on the water. If only life could be so simple.

"Hey, look at all those stars! Must be the Milky Way, don't you think?" Logan lay on his back and gazed at the sky.

"It's beautiful." Lindsay lay beside him and looked up.

The moon slid behind a cloud and the air began to cool. Lindsay realized she was cold, lying on the ground, and sat up.

"Guess we'd better turn in and get rested up for tomorrow. We want to have plenty of energy to hike along the ridge and see all the great rock formations."

Lindsay brushed her teeth, using a cup of water to rinse her mouth. She splashed water on her face. She noticed that Logan did not brush his teeth, but thought one night probably wouldn't matter.

The three of them crawled into their sleeping bags, with Dad in the middle of the tent and Lindsay on one side and Logan on the other. Logan fell asleep almost as soon as he lay down, and soon she heard her dad snoring softly. But Lindsay lay there awake, thinking about the day and whether anything would change when they got back home.

Lindsay woke suddenly. She shivered and pulled her sleeping bag up over her nose. A root poked her in the back as she rolled over. It was dark and still inside the tent, and she wondered what time it was. A shriek pierced the silence.

"What's that?!"

"An owl, probably. Go to sleep." Dad rolled over and began to snore.

Lindsay heard a soft plop and then another on the outside the tent. She felt the side of the tent and could tell it was damp. She moved closer to her dad and went back to sleep.

When Lindsay opened her eyes, a dim light filtered into the tent. Pots clanked outside, and she smelled the smoke of a campfire. It smelled reassuring.

"Hey, get up. Time for breakfast." Logan tapped on the side of the tent.

Lindsay groaned. When she exhaled, she could see her breath. Inside her sleeping bag, she put on her jacket and an extra pair of socks. She unzipped her sleeping bag, laced her boots, and unzipped the tent door.

"Yuk! It snowed last night! But it's still October!"

"No kidding." Logan was attempting to keep a fire going, but the wet wood puffed more smoke than fire.

"Where's Dad?"

"He climbed down that bank to see if he could find some wood that stayed drier under the trees." Dad's head appeared over the bank and then disappeared again.

"Need some help?" called Logan.

"Just need to get my footing." Dad's head appeared again, and then his arms flailed, and they heard a thud as he slid out of sight.

"Umph." Then silence.

"Dad?" Lindsay and Logan ran to the edge of the bank. Dad lay on his back with his leg twisted underneath him. They scrambled down the bank.

"Dad, are you okay?" Lindsay knelt beside him. "Come on, let's help him up."

Lindsay and Logan put their arms under his shoulders and pulled him up. He stood on one foot and carefully placed his right foot on the ground.

"Ouch! I can't stand on my ankle." He sat back down. Lindsay and Logan knelt beside him, not sure what to do.

After a few minutes, Lindsay looked at his ankle. "It looks swollen. We should ice it, but we don't have any ice."

"Call 911 on your cell phone," Logan suggested, "so we can get an ambulance out here."

Dad grimaced. "I didn't bring a cell phone. Out in the wilds and all that."

"You didn't?" Logan frowned. "Why would you go anywhere without your cell phone?" He shook his head.

"Wait, Mom gave me her cell phone, just in case. Let's help him up the bank, so we can keep him warm, and I'll call Mom."

"Just in case what?" said her dad, but Lindsay didn't answer.

Logan grabbed a gnarled stick and handed it to his dad. With Dad leaning on it, the three of them edged up the bank. Logan dragged Dad's sleeping bag out of the tent. Dad sat down and pulled off his shoe. Lindsay ran to the tent, pulled the cell phone out of her backpack, and flipped it open. She shook her head. "There's no signal out here."

"No signal?" Logan looked skeptical. "This really is out in the wild."

"So," said Lindsay, "someone has to go back to the campground for help. I'll go."

"No, you stay with Dad. I can go faster than you."

"You'll both go then. I'm not letting one of you go alone." Dad shook his head.

"Someone has to stay with you. You can't get around, and you have to stay warm. You could go into shock." Logan frowned.

"You're such a Boy Scout." Lindsay shook her head. "But you're probably right."

"Lindsay can stay with you, and I'll go back as fast as I can."

"No, I don't like it. Something could happen." Dad shook his head again.

"Nothing's going to happen. It's not that far. It didn't take that long to get here, and without a pack it will be a lot faster."

"It seemed far to me," Lindsay mumbled."

"I don't know. I don't like it." Dad frowned.

But Logan was already putting his water bottle, some snacks, and his compass into his empty day pack. He set his red hat on his head and set off down the trail. "I'll be back in a few hours with help," he called back, and was soon out of sight.

"Logan," Dad called and tried to get up. He groaned and slid back down.

"Don't worry, Dad. Logan is a real Boy Scout. He knows his way in the woods. Do you think some of that wood you were looking for might be drier? Then the fire wouldn't smoke like that?"

"I had a pile of sticks and a couple of small logs that I pulled out from underneath the trees, but then I slipped when I started to bring it up."

Lindsay climbed down into the hollow and brought up a stack of sticks. She went back and brought back a couple of larger logs. When she came back to the fire, Dad was feeding sticks one at a time.

"Blow on it a bit."

Lindsay bent down and blew several times as hard as she could. Shoots of little flames struggled up, and soon there was a small fire. When it got bigger, Lindsay put on one of the smaller logs.

"Hey, that's better."

"Maybe we could make something for breakfast." Lindsay got up and rummaged in Dad's pack. She held up the oatmeal.

"Bring me that little cookstove, and I'll show you how to start it. It'll take no time at all to boil up some water and cook that oatmeal. There's brown sugar in there and some powdered milk."

Lindsay followed Dad's instructions and, when the stove was lit, set a pot of water on. Sitting side by side, they ate oatmeal and used leftover water to make instant coffee. Lindsay grimaced a bit when she tasted the coffee, but it warmed her. As she rinsed the dishes and put things away, the sun peaked out behind the clouds, and patches of blue began to seep across the sky.

Logan strode quickly down the trail. He did feel a bit anxious, worried he would get lost, or not find anyone to help. But he also loved being out in the woods by himself. He loved the smell of the pines and the rat-a-tat of a woodpecker. The crunch of the leaves under his feet.

He knew he had to get help for his dad, and hoped he would find a ranger when he got to the parking area. Or somebody with a phone at least. He hoped Lindsay and their dad would get along okay while he was gone. Maybe things could get back to normal after they got home. Maybe Dad would visit them every other weekend. Maybe his mom and dad would get along and not argue.

Boy Scout camping trips had taught him to watch for landmarks, so he would never be lost. He remembered that big oak next to the trail. They had passed it soon after they left the parking area, so he was getting close.

He took a deep breath when he spotted the parked cars. He had made it! He looked around, but the cars were all emp-ty. He did not see anyone getting in or out of one. For a mo-

ment he panicked. What would he do if he couldn't find anyone?

Then he took a deep breath. He was in luck, because there
was a ranger checking the cars for park passes. He ran up to
him and the ranger looked up.

"It's my dad. He may have broken his leg. Anyway, he
can't walk, and someone needs to come and fix his leg or help
get him back to the car."

"Okay. Slow down a bit. Where is your dad?"

"We're camped near Chapel Rock. We backpacked there
yesterday. But this morning Dad tried to find some dry firewood, and he fell down the hill. Now he can't walk."

"I'll call my partner. He's cutting some tree limbs a half
mile down the road. We'll come with you and see how bad it
is. We have a collapsible cart, if needed." The ranger took out
his phone and alerted his partner.

Logan nodded. He paced around the parking lot, waiting
for the guy to come. In a few minutes the other ranger drove
up, got out of his vehicle, and pulled a folded cart from the
back of it.

"All right, lead the way." The ranger gestured to the trail,
and Logan set off at a brisk pace. As they walked, the ranger
asked a few more questions about Logan's dad and the accident, but mostly they walked in silence.

"Hey," said Dad. "That sun will melt off this little bit of snow and warm things up."

Lindsay nodded.

"There's a pack of cards in my pack. How about Crazy Eights? You loved that game when you were little. Maybe because you always beat Logan when you played it." Dad grinned at her.

"Did I?"

After five games of Crazy Eights, of which Lindsay won four, Lindsay and her dad sat quietly.

"I brought a book I have to read for English class. I could read some of it to you."

Dad nodded. "That'd pass the time."

Lindsay read a chapter, put the book down and leaned against her dad. He put his arm around her.

"Tell me a romantic story."

"There was a king who had the most beautiful daughter."

"Your stories always have daughters."

"Well, there's nothing like having a daughter. Anyway, this king didn't always do the right thing, but he meant well. And he loved his daughter more than anything."

"Hey, you guys okay?" Lindsay jumped up at the sound of the deep voice and whirled around.

"Dad, Lindsay. See, I told you I'd be back soon!" Logan ran out of the woods and over to them. Two rangers in uniform followed him.

Lindsay hugged Logan, and he laughed. "Hey, nice fire."

"You're not the only one who knows how to build a fire, you know."

"Looks like you did a real job on that ankle." The ranger knelt down by Dad and looked at his foot.

"'fraid so."

"You're lucky to have such able youngsters around." The ranger nodded at Logan and Lindsay.

"I am. Can't get along without them."

"I'll put an ice pack on that ankle to take down some of the swelling. We'll help you pack up this camp and pull you in the cart out to the road. You know, there's a two-track path just a hundred yards from here, so it won't take long. We'll call for a truck to meet us at the road"

"Thanks. I appreciate it. Sorry to put you to all this trouble."

"No problem."

When everything was packed, the rangers helped Dad into the cart, and they followed the path through the trees out to the waiting truck. Lindsay began to whistle. Logan, grinning, walked beside her.

FUN FACTS:

Is there a Chapel Rock on Lake Superior?

Yes, it is part of Pictured Rocks National Lakeshore on the shore of Lake Michigan in the Upper Peninsula. It is a remnant of Cambrian Age Sandstone and was carved 3800 years ago. There are many interesting rock formations along the shoreline. You can see them by hiking or taking a trip on a ferry boat.

(nps.gov/places/chapel-rock.htm)

How large is Lake Superior?

A glacial lake, it is the largest freshwater lake in the world by surface area and the third largest by volume. The average depth is 483 feet. The Ojibwa name for it is gichi-gami.

(wikipedia.org/wiki/Lake_Superior)

Virtual Vacation

"Come on, Marsa, finish packing. Mom says our autopod will be here any minute." Com stood in the doorway and watched his younger sister.

"Almost done." Marsa looked at herself in the large video screen on the wall. She touched the icon pad, changing the reflection of herself wearing yellow shorts and a light blue shirt to a short, flared skirt with a red tee shirt. "What do you think?"

"Just pick one. It doesn't matter what you wear. No one will notice."

"I get to choose where we go this year." Marsa smiled.

"I know. Don't pick anything babyish."

"I'm not a baby."

"Time to go." At the sound of her voice, their mother's face appeared on the screen.

"Coming." Marsa spoke toward the image on the screen, and Mom's face faded. She touched the icon pad for both outfits and the suitcase button. She heard the familiar whir as the suitcase slid down the chute from the closet. She opened the closet door and watched as the metal arms pulled the outfits off the hangars, folded them, and put them in the suitcase. She clicked the remote to close the suitcase and send it rolling out of the room, down the hall to the front door.

Com and Marsa stood on the front porch of their house with their parents. Exactly at 9:00 am, the sleek aluminum autopod zoomed up to the landing pad beside the house, beeped, and the doors opened.

Dad and Mom settled into the front seat, while Marsa and Com climbed into the back. Dad entered the coordinates of their destination on the smooth, flat icon pad and the autopod zoomed off. Touching another icon on the pad, he began to read the news. Mom touched the icon pad in front of her too, and found her place in the book she was reading.

Com selected his favorite music videos. Marsa gazed out the window as the autopod rose higher in the bright blue sky. She could see the tops of the tallest buildings as other autopods cruised past them in different directions.

Marsa's phone beeped, and she looked down at the text message from her brother. "So, where are we going? What did you choose?"

"You'll see," Marsa said. She looked over at her brother, but he was nodding along to the sounds from the ear buds. Marsa typed, "Don't you want to know what I chose?"

Com shrugged and tapped his fingers to a song.

The autopod landed in front of a large, blue, domed building. "You have arrived. When you exit your autopod, please punch in #A72 for parking," intoned the voice from the speaker. Dad held his phone up to the pad for a notice of the parking number.

"I knew you'd choose this."

"Did not."

"Here we are." When they all got out, Dad punched in #A72 and the autopod slid off.

Standing beside her dad, Marsa looked up at the neon sign that flashed across the front of the dome, Virtuality Extravaganza. "I've always wanted to come here."

"For at least all of your ten years." Mom smiled.

"I like Virtuality and You better, I think." Com frowned.

"You'll like this, you'll see."

Dad lined up at one of the pay screens, while the rest of the family scanned the list of possible adventures.

"Marsa, which one are you going to choose?" Mom looked up from the screen she was reading.

"Either Super Girl or Little Mermaid. I want to either fly or swim underwater. What about you, Mom?"

"I think Pride and Prejudice. I've always wanted to meet Mr. Darcy. Com?"

"I'm going on tour with the Space Invaders. I want to see what it was like when bands played guitars and sang into microphones."

"What do you think Dad will choose?" Marsa looked at her mom.

"I'll bet either Spider-Man or Batman."

"Which will you be, Dad, Spider-Man or Batman?" Marsa looked at her dad.

"Probably Batman. I'm feeling more like driving a hot car than climbing buildings."

"Drive carefully." Marsa frowned.

"It's not for real." Com shook his head.

"But it'll feel real. I guess I'll do Little Mermaid. I like the water, and I love to sing."

They each touched the icons for their choices and scanned their thumbprints. They joined the crowd at the helepod doors and waited for the car that would take them to the right level. Only a certain number of people could ride at any one time, and when that number was reached, an invisible barrier stopped more people from entering. Marsa was glad the helepod car was never overly crowded.

"I'm on #5."

"I'm #6."

"Dad and I are on #7 and #8. Com, when yours is over, wait for Marsa. We'll all meet in the Virtual Café for lunch at 12:30."

Dad smiled. "Let's roll."

The doors slid open, and they stepped into the helepod, shaped like a large sausage. They punched in the levels where they were going, and the helepod soared upward. Marsa watched the number of the floors flash by on the screen. Com got off at #5, and she got off at level #6 and got in line at the door to the Little Mermaid Adventure. A girl just ahead of her, who looked about her age, turned around and smiled at her.

"Hi, I'm Aurora. Have you been here before?"

"Oh, hi. I'm Marsa. This is my first time. My brother likes Virtuality and You, so we went there last year. What about you?"

"I did this one last year. Are you going to choose wet or dry?"

"Wet. It feels more like the real thing. You?"

"Definitely wet. Hey, since we're next to each other in line, we'll be in booths next to each other."

"Yeah."

"So, we could do the Little Mermaid together."

"How would we do that?" Marsa smiled at the idea.

"We could each put on our headsets, get into the same booth, follow along at the same pace, share what happens."

"Okay." Marsa wasn't sure how that worked, but it sounded fun.

Aurora was now at the front of the line, and the voice overhead said, "Please enter Booth C." She entered the booth, which had a railing separating it from the next booth. She waited until Marsa entered the booth next to her. Marsa gave Aurora a thumbs up.

The voice overhead said, "Please put on your headset and follow the directions."

Marsa put on her headset and touched Start. She looked over at Aurora and saw she had done the same. She moved over so that Aurora could fit into her booth.

"Choose wet or dry." Marisa chose wet. The mist felt cold at first, but she soon got used to it. She breathed in the salty smell of the ocean and dove through the water, flapping her tail back and forth. Swimming with a tail wasn't as easy as it looked.

Aurora was swimming, too. She nudged Marsa and laughed. Marsa laughed back.

Marisa looked at all of her treasures lined up on the rocks on the floor of the ocean and began to sing. When she ended with "part of that world," she was talking with a crab. And then King Triton was there, and he was upset with her. Marsa shivered a little. He seemed kind of big and scary. Her sisters always did as their father wanted, but Ariel seemed to make him angry a lot. The prince was very handsome, but she felt a little dizzy after the little boat they were in spun around and around. It was difficult, not being able to talk. There were so many things she wanted to say. Oh, no, here came that evil Ursula who looked like the Little Mermaid but really wasn't.

"Uh, oh, here comes the evil Ursula," Aurora whispered.

"Just be careful." Marsa whispered and watched the screen. She opened her mouth, but nothing came out, and she couldn't warn the prince in time! When Ursula towered over them and her voice boomed out, Marsa screamed.

Aurora screamed, too, and they both shivered. After Ursula was defeated, Marsa collapsed with exhaustion. That was hard work. She grinned at Aurora, and Aurora grinned back.

Marsa felt grownup and elegant, wearing the white satin dress at the wedding. The flowers in her bouquet smelled lovely. She sighed when the wedding ended and smiled at Aurora. "Please wait while you dry off." A fan of warm air began to blow on them gently. They both took off their headsets and walked toward the exit.

"That was fun. We should do that again."

"Agreed." Aurora nodded. "Which one are you doing after lunch?"

"Rainforest. You?"

"I'll do the same. Meet you there."

Com strummed the guitar and tried to keep up with the band. Colorful lights blinked on and off, and the music blared loudly. These electric guitars were heavier than he thought they would be, and his fingers felt awkward and stiff. Maybe that's why now they do it all on computer. Still, the crowd was screaming, and they seemed to love him and the band. Hearing his voice over the microphone echoing around the big arena surprised him, and he lost his place in the song for a minute. Now he was back on track, and the crowd wanted an encore. During the encore, Com tried leaping into the air with his guitar like some of the guys in the band. He caught himself as he nearly fell. He wouldn't try that one again! When the set was finished, he wanted a break, but the band had to pack up everything and catch an airplane for the next performance. Taking an airplane was a real hassle, a lot of lugging baggage around and standing in lines.

Mom looked into Darcy's eyes. My, he was handsome. But maybe a tad too stiff. He didn't seem to have much of a sense of humor. Still, he was tall, dark, and handsome, and very wealthy. She could have spent her entire time just going through his grand estate. The furnishings were elegant, but not too practical for a family. She wished she could take home that chair by the window. It would look lovely in the living room. And that vase of flowers smelled divine. If only she could grow roses like that! It was romantic when Darcy finally admitted he'd been a bit of a jerk and proposed to her.

Dad studied himself in the mirror. Maybe he was a little stout for Batman. The Batmobile zoomed up and he climbed in. "Place your hands on the steering wheel," said a deep voice. Dad looked at the round wheel directly in front of him and placed his hands on it. There were all kinds of buttons, and he tried them all out. When he touched the gas pedal, the car lurched forward, and he sped right toward a brick wall. "Turn the wheel," said the voice. "No, not to the right, to the left." Oh, no, he was going to crash! Just in time, Dad wrenched the wheel to the left and the Batmobile zoomed around a corner. Close call.

Marsa stood outside #6 waiting for Com. Aurora waited beside her for her mom to come and pick her up.

"You ready?" Com stood in front of her. "Mom and Dad will be waiting."

"Hey, Com, this is Aurora. She's a really experienced mermaid."

"Hi." Aurora looked at Com, then back at Marsa. "Your hair is still a little damp. It'll dry, I guess."

"So, I'll see you at the Rainforest."

Aurora nodded.

"Okay. See you."

"You had fun?" Com looked at Marsa.

"It was great. You?"

"Yeah, pretty cool."

Com headed off toward the helepod that would take them to the Virtual Café. He took out his I phone and began texting. Marsa hurried after her brother, turned and waved to Aurora.

At the Virtual Café, they stepped onto the moving pathway that took them to the Food Booth. Marsa looked into the eye scanner and a voice said, "Please place your order now." She entered the information about her height, weight, and age and then touched pictures of a veggie burger and salad. She moved on to the Food Slot as the tray slid down in front of her.

"Hey, you must be growing." Com looked in appreciation at Marisa's tray. "They gave you a bigger burger this time."

"You're right." Marsa smiled. Someday, she might even be taller than Com.

At the table, Dad was already tuned in to the sports update while he forked salad into his mouth. Mom was reading her book. Com turned up his ear pod to hear a message from one of his friends. Marsa spotted Aurora across the room, waited until she looked toward her, then waved. Aurora smiled and waved back.

After lunch, Marsa and her family headed back to the Selection Room.

"So, what are you doing this afternoon?" Mom scanned the list of choices.

"I'm going to the rainforest," said Marsa.

"Great idea. My grandmother went to a real one and actually walked through it."

"We know, Mom." Com rolled his eyes. "It must have been hot and damp, and she must have worried about real snakes and stuff."

"Wouldn't that be cool? There might be real birds and animals. I wouldn't be scared at all." Marsa touched the screen for Level #4.

"Could be dangerous."

"But wouldn't it be great to see a real leopard up in a tree or see a flock of colored parrots and hear what they sound like. You could sit under one of those giant leaves and feel the air on your face. Or smell one of those tropical flowers. I'll bet they smell different when they're real."

"Maybe." Com looked at her and shook his head.

"My friend Aurora is going to do the Rainforest, too."

Mom looked at her, puzzled, but didn't say anything. "I'm going to climb the Himalayan Mountains."

Marsa looked at her in awe. "Wow. Be careful."

Her mother smiled. "I will."

"What about you, Dad?"

"I'm going to visit the penguins in Antarctica."

"Oh, cool."

Dad laughed. "Probably quite cool. I brought my jacket, though. Well, let's get going," said Dad. "Better catch the next helepod."

Marsa waited for Aurora outside the virtual room. A few minutes later, Aurora ran up to her.

"You ready?"

Marsa nodded. "Can't wait." When their booth numbers were called, they put on their headsets and squeezed into Aurora's booth.

The warm, moist air tickled Marsa's arms, and she looked up at the towering green trees. Along the path that drew her deeper into the forest, she spied brilliantly colored flowers nestled beneath the trees. She breathed in the sweet, tangy air. Vanilla, maybe, and something else. Suddenly, she heard a faint rustling behind a tree. Aurora heard it, too, and grabbed Marsa's hand.

Marsa almost stopped breathing as a sleek black panther, at least six feet long not including the tail, slipped out from among the leaves. He stood and looked at her and then slunk quietly away. "Wow!" said Marsa and nudged Aurora. Aurora nodded.

As they walked further, the trail seemed to wind upward. A rope hanging near her face began to sway. Marsa reached up to swat it aside, just as she saw the snakeskin that covered it. She shrieked, grabbed Aurora's hand, and dashed on down the path. Turning back, they watched the snake slither back up onto a branch.

"Was that a boa constrictor?" Marisa whispered.

"Maybe."

When they reached the top of the path, they came upon a platform with a wire that was connected from one tree to another. "You have reached the Zipline. Please step into the harness. No, not that way, one leg on each side. Please fasten the clip to the wire as shown on the diagram. Yes, that's correct."

Marsa followed the directions and waited. She looked over at Aurora and saw that she was clipped on, too. She felt a nudge and was sailing down the zipline. They both gasped as the next tree arose before them, but they automatically slowed down and were set upon the platform.

"Please unclip yourself and step out of the harness. Thank you."

Marsa and Aurora left the virtual room and waited in the hall.

"Hey, wasn't that cool?"

"Did you see the snake?"

"I touched it before I realized what it was. If it'd been real, I might not be here." Aurora laughed. "You've got a leaf in your hair."

"So do you."

Com hefted the bats to see which one he wanted to use. These pro team bats were heavier than the one his team used. He swung it back and forth. He heard his name as the speaker announced the batter up, and he stepped up to the plate. He smelled peanuts and something fried.

"The wind up, and the pitch." The ball whizzed over the plate and smacked into the catcher's mitt before Com could swing. Strike one. It happened again for strike two. But on the third pitch he swung the bat, it connected with a loud thwack. It was over the fence! Com trotted around the bases for a home run. When he got to home plate, the people clapped and shouted his name. Com grinned and waved to the crowd. Batting should always be this easy.

Mom put on her headset, and hooked up the ropes that would keep her from falling. She headed toward the mountain with a few other climbers, following the Sherpas who would lead them. At the base of the mountain, the Sherpas stopped and gave them all the safety instructions that they should follow. Mom took a deep breath. The mountain top looked very far away. Slowly, they climbed, single file. The air was icy cold, but smelled fresh. Breathing was more difficult in the thinner air. Sometimes the Sherpas helped to haul them up to the next level. Part of the time, everyone crept along the edge of a cliff. Mom looked down once to see how deep the crevasse was, and tried not to look down again. At one point, she slipped and tumbled over the side. She closed her eyes, but reached out and was able to plunge her ice axe into the snow. I'm going to die, she thought! Then shook herself back to reality. She would only die virtually. The Sherpas pulled her back up, and she made it to the top. The views were extraordinary!

Dad put on his headset and boarded the boat that would take him around Antarctica to see the penguins. Ocean, snow and ice were all he could see for miles. Whales breached the water or swam close to the boat. A whale like that could capsize them! It was quiet except for the sound of the waves washing against the boat. Finally, they reached the shore, where they could see hundreds of penguins: large ones, medium ones, baby ones. They got off the boat and walked among them. The air was cold, and he could see his breath. Dad sat on a chunk of ice and the penguins crowded around him. He reached out to pet one, but it ducked away. Then they were called back to the boat, which brought them back to where they started.

Com walked up to Marsa and Aurora. "Ready to find Mom and Dad? They'll be wanting to get going."

"Give me your phone number. I'll text you sometime." Marsa handed Aurora her phone. Aurora smiled and typed in her number.

Com took Marsa's arm and pulled her toward the hele-pod. Marsa turned and waved to Aurora.

"You can't just give out your number to people you don't know." Com shook his head.

"I know her now." Marsa smiled.

FUN FACTS:

Are people able to take virtual trips?

Yes. Virtual reality (VR) simulates experience using displays and movement tracking to give users a feel of "being there." Virtual reality techniques are found in entertainment, education, and elsewhere. Multi-screen movie theaters, flight and driving simulators, and video games pioneered the field. Travel is another application.

Today's virtual reality systems use headsets or sound and image projectors to simulate a user's physical presence in an environment. The techniques described in the story are more sophisticated than anything currently available.

(wikipedia.org/wiki/Virtual_reality)

What kind of snake is a boa constrictor?

Boa constructors live in Central and South America. The patterns of their skin vary depending on their habitat. Adults can be thirteen feet long and weigh more than one hundred pounds. They wrap around their prey and squeeze their muscles to subdue them. Boas seldom attack humans, as even human babies are too large to be prey.

(nationalzoo.si.edu/animals/boa-constrictor, Smithsonian National Zoo and Conservation Biology Institute)

The Best Summer Vacation Ever

Last summer, I was really lucky because Mom and Dad and I visited Costa Rica for a whole week. We stayed in this really cool hotel where we had a big room on the side of the hill, and we could sit out on our own patio and see across the ocean for miles and miles. The water was so blue it made your eyes hurt.

And one thing that is great about CR is the weather. The sun shines every day in a bright, blue sky, and it never rains, not even once. In the middle of the afternoon, it gets pretty hot, but then you can just walk down to the beach and cool off in the ocean. The place we stayed at also had a swimming pool, so sometimes we swam there, too.

The second day we were there, we took this tour down a river through the jungle and got to see all kinds of cool animals and birds. There were three kinds of monkey swinging from the trees, and the biggest crocodiles you ever saw, swimming around in the river or sunning themselves on the riverbanks. This one humongous crocodile swam right up to the side of the boat where I was sitting and looked right at me. This boy next to me thought I'd be scared but, of course, I wasn't scared at all. Our guide did say it isn't a good idea to feed them, so we didn't.

We saw a whole flock of these funny birds called roseate spoonbills. I've seen lots of pink flamingos before, but these spoonbills are pink and white with these spoon-like bills, so they can scoop fish right out of the water. We must have seen a hundred of them.

The day after that, we went to the rainforest and rode the zipline through the trees. I don't know if you have ever heard of one of these before, but it's a wire that's strung between the trees, and you sit in a sling, and they hook it right up to the wire and give you a push. If you don't hold down too hard on the wire with your hand, you go zipping real fast down that wire. And if you forget to slow yourself down, you could whack right into the next tree. Some of the wires gave us a really long ride, and then you can look down and see what's underneath those tall trees. I saw two leopards laying underneath one of those trees, a lion underneath another one, and a whole herd of gazelles bounding through the jungle. That was a pretty cool ride, and the guy who was our guide said I was probably the fastest zipper he had ever seen.

The next day we decided not to go on any tours, but just to drive into the village nearby and do some shopping. We went into this really cool little store and I bought a whistle shaped like a toucan. Then, when we left the store, I looked across the street, and you won't believe who I saw. I didn't believe it at first, either. This famous actor. He was filming a movie right there in CR across the street from where I was standing. I asked Mom if we could watch, and she thought it would be okay.

Not only was it okay, but the actor himself saw us standing there, and he asked me if I wanted a part in his movie. The kid who was supposed to be in the movie had gotten really sick, and they wanted to go ahead and shoot those scenes. At first I thought he was joking with me, but then the director came over, and before I knew what was happening, I was riding on a motorcycle down a dirt road to the ocean (this village is right on the coast) where we pretended we were surfing some really big waves. I never had so much fun in my life, and they said next time they're in Ann Arbor, they'll look me up. I can't remember the name of the movie, but it'll be out sometime soon, so watch for me in it.

As if that weren't enough excitement, the next night when we walked over to the hotel for dinner, everyone was in a big uproar because some lady's expensive diamond bracelet was missing, and she thought it was stolen. The hotel manager was trying to calm her down, but she just kept crying. So, I started looking around and, sure enough, I found that bracelet. She must have been looking into the fountain in the courtyard, because that bracelet was winking at me from the bottom of it. I scooped it out and asked was this hers. She let out a whoop and grabbed me up in a big hug. She couldn't thank me enough and was so grateful that she paid for my family's hotel bill for the entire week. My parents were proud as can be and, of course, pretty happy about the free stay.

On the next to the last day, we decided to just relax because we were going to have to go home the following day. In the morning, I listened to the howler monkeys in the trees down by the beach and read for a while, and watched a couple of little crabs scuttle across our patio. My Mom didn't like them too much because she was afraid they would get into our room, but I thought they were kind of cute.

In the afternoon, we went down to the beach. My dad and I rented kayaks and paddled around near shore. There's kind of a cove there by the hotel, so we didn't have to worry about big waves or something. While I was paddling, I heard someone yell "help, help, my baby." I looked toward shore, and there was a woman jumping up and down and pointing. I looked where she was pointing, and there was a little kid thrashing around out in the deep water. He wasn't really a baby, but he wasn't very big either. I didn't even think much about it, but just jumped right out of the kayak and swam as hard as I could toward that little guy. His head bobbed under once before I got there, but I grabbed him real tight and swam for all I was worth toward shore. His Mom was really glad to get him back. She kept calling me a hero and told the hotel manager and all so that he called the local TV station, and they came out and interviewed me. The mayor even came and gave me a medal. Unfortunately, I lost the medal somewhere. It must have come loose and slid off.

So, the next day we had to go home. I didn't really mind. It was definitely the best vacation I've ever had, but I was kind of ready to go home.

And that's how I spent my summer vacation.

Ethan Campbell

Mrs. Emory's 4th grade

FUN FACTS:

Where is Costa Rica?

Costa Rica is a Central American country with coastlines on the Caribbean and on the Pacific Ocean. The country has three mountain ranges that include active volcanoes, rainforests and cloud forests, and large waterfalls. One quarter of its area is protected jungles. The capital is San Juan.

(www.visitcostarica.com)

What animals live in Costa Rica?

There are no leopards, lions, our gazelles in Costa Rica. There are crocodiles, rosetted spoonbills, and howler monkeys. There are also jaguars, ocelots, pumas, tapirs, and sloths.

Acknowledgments

Many thanks to the following:

The Society for Children's Book Writers and Illustrators (SCBWI), Michigan Chapter for the many things I learned about writing for children.

My first critique group: Mary Gallagher, Elsa, Sharon Blankenship, Lisa Patrell, and Claudia Boschitz who critiqued my stories and encouraged me to write.

Melanie Gorzonio for taking the time to read these stories and offer her helpful insights. Also, for her suggestion to include FUN FACTS.

My parents and sister for sharing my first family vacations and how much fun they could be.

Briana Chalker for the title of the book, consultation on the cover, and all the fun she added to our family vacations.

Peter Solenberger for reading the stories and offering insights, taking care of the many technical tasks required to produce this book, and for supporting and encouraging me during the writing and producing process. And, of course, for sharing many fun family vacations.

Most of the cover images are by the author. The 1925 Ford Model T Touring Car is from ModelTMitch, cc-by-sa-4.0, via Wikimedia Commons. The postcard of Camel's Hump and Winooski River, Green Mountains, Vermont, is from the Boston Public Library, cc-by-2.0, via Wikimedia Commons. The flourish at the beginning of each story is from publicdomainvectors.org.

About the Author

Dawn Chalker loves to travel and has based many of these stories on locations where she vacationed with her family. She has visited all fifty states, as well as Canada, Europe, and Latin America. Exploring the natural environment and wildlife is often part of her travels. Unfortunately, she has never met a dragon. She lives in Leelanau County, Michigan, and writes novels and stories for kids and adults.